# SIN IS A TRILLION DOLLAR INDUSTRY

# SIN IS A TRILLION DOLLAR INDUSTRY

*Its All About Business*

Jamella A. Jihad

**To order additional copies of this book, contact:**
Xlibris
1-888-795-4274
www.Xlibris.com
Orders@Xlibris.com
543795

# Contents

# Dedication

I dedicate this book to my wonderful husband, Imam, and friend: thank you, Siraj, for being supportive of my work, for being a wonderful husband and father. Thank you for the many sacrifices you have made for your family and community, and thank you for your devotion to Islam and for spreading this deen of Allah. I truly appreciate your teachings, your love for family life and community life, and most of all, your love for Allah Subhaana WaTa'ala and Prophet Muhammad (PBUH). Your many attributes that manifest in your character and your actions have helped me to be a better wife, mother, grandmother, and person in Al-Islam. May Allah bless you with the highest level of Al-Jannah. Ameen!

To my wonderful children, Abdus-Samaad, Aisha, Nardin, Inshirah, Baiyina, and Muhammad Jihad, thank you for your love, faithfulness, and loyalty and for being good Muslims. May Allah forever guide and protect you. May He bless you with the good in this life and with the highest level of Al-Jannah. Ameen!

To Gloria (Granny), thank you for being such a wonderful mother-in-law and for being supportive; may Allah continue to give you good health, a long life and continue to bless and guide you. And to my Wahhaj family, may Allah continue to guide, protect, and bless you with the good of this life, the good of the next, and Al-Jannah. Ameen!

And to my wonderful sister Gwen and my brothers Andre and Khabir, thank you for your love and support. May

Allah guide you and protect you and bless you with all the good in this life and the next. Ameen!

To Shikina and Kiara (KeKe), thank you for your love and for being such wonderful nieces. May Allah continue to guide, protect, and bless you with the good of this life and the next. Ameen!

And to my Christian family members, thank you for being loyal and faithful. Thank you for your love and support. May Allah continue to guide, protect, and bless you with the good of both worlds!

A message for my grandchildren: may Allah bless each of you to grow up to be righteous children, to live moral lives, and to die as believers. Always hold on to your faith. Keep Allah out front, and never sway from Him; He will be there for you even when you're not there for yourself. Never give up on Allah. These are the words I echo from your great-grandmother Joann Reid.

To my dear wonderful friends—you know who you are— smile. Thank you for your love and support. May Allah continue to guide, protect, and bless you with the good of both worlds.

Thank you Hajja Rasheedah Shamsid-Deen, Sister Ayesha Safeeullah and Brother Samuel Shareef for your assistance in editing this book, may Allah bless you with the good of this life and in the hereafter.

# Foreword

In The Name of Allah, The Most Merciful and Mercy Giving Surah Al-Falaq (The Day Break) Holy Qur'an Chapter 113 (CXIII)

1. Say "I seek refuge with (Allah) the Lord of the Day-Break,
2. From the evil of what He has created;
3. And from the evil of the darkening (night) as it comes with its darkness; (or the moon as it sets or goes away)
4. And from the evil of the witchcrafts when they blow in the knots.
5. And from the evil of the envier when he envies."

Many people ask the question, "What is my purpose in this life?" Many individuals who ask this question search for their purpose in this life, while others take life for granted. Some of us have not been able to come up with the answer to this question. I used to ask myself this same question for many years. After years of trying to find contentment in many projects that I either personally developed or have worked on with others, I can honestly say without a shadow of a doubt that my true purpose in this life is to serve and worship Allah and to be kind and helpful to humanity. Nothing brings me greater joy than knowing that I have helped someone find their way, even if it's just by putting a smile on their face.

My work will be completed when I return to Allah Almighty, and I pray that He accepts my labor and good deeds; truly I am striving for Al Jannah (Paradise)! Nowadays, mentioning Allah's name (which Allah means "God" in Arabic) doesn't sit too well with wrongdoers; they will always have a problem with us using or saying "Allah." Sinners do not want you to mention Allah/God's name in business transactions and politics. Truthfully, Sinners don't want you to ever mention God's name regarding their bad behaviors. You will hear many say, "God has nothing to do with it." For wrongdoers, it's about building wealth, and if they cannot make money off God's name, they want others to forget or erase their faith, religion, and belief in God and to keep it out of their minds and their day-to-day activities.

And if they can become billionaires off of God's name and His creation, then it will still not be enough; greed will still force them to go against God's laws.

The purpose of this book is to help encourage those individuals who want to go into business to do so without risking their relationship with God. I will say to you, as with any business, we must have faith, trust, and belief that we can have lawful businesses that will help us in this life, and that will benefit us in the next life. You must believe in yourself and the Creator of all the Worlds, to succeed in life and business.

Developing a business in this society and keeping a healthy and faithful lifestyle is work; never think operating your own business will be easy especially when dealing with other human beings.

There will always be obstacles we all must go through and overcome, not just in business but in everything we do. Your mindset is to know; whatever you do in this life is only temporary, and you will not be able to take this business with you when you die, but you can leave a good legacy behind that will be of benefit to you in the next life.

There are some people who cannot accept it when they fail or if they do not meet their goals that they have set for themselves. In cases like this, people will lose hope and faith in Allah. In cases like this people have allowed what is only temporary to destroy their lives and all their good deeds. It is a proven fact that most people have the tendency of putting business before Allah and their family. When a person puts their business before Allah, I can tell you only from experience that it will not be successful, even if you're making all the money you believe you have made. Additionally, when you put your business before family, eventually you will find your family unhappy even though you feel you have provided them with all the money and material things. To avoid ruining yourself, your marriage, your family, and your business, you must put all these priorities in their proper places.

We only want the best for our fellow businesspeople who seek success in business! May this small book help those who want to fulfill their desire in succeeding in life and business the lawful way!

With the help of Allah, and with His guidance and your faith in Him, you can succeed in your endeavors in this life.

Important translations

Allah is an Arabic term which means "God" Therefore; you will know I am talking about the One Creator when you see it. Most non-Muslims believe Allah is some other god that is worshiped. However in Arabic speaking countries like in the Middle East, Christian Arabs, Jews, and other citizens say "Allah" when referring to The One Creator.

PBUH stands for "peace be upon him"; so you will see PBUH after we mention Muhammad the Prophet PBUH or any of God's Prophets including any references to them as a sign of respect.

Al Jannah is an Arabic term which means "Paradise."

Halal is the Arabic term meaning "lawful."

Haram is the Arabic term meaning "unlawful or forbidden."

Nafs is the Arabic term for one's "self-desires."

# Introduction

According to *Business Insider*, there are 28 million businesses today, and over 22 million of these are self-employed. The majority of these businesses started from an idea. The key to an *IDEA* is making it a reality.

I thought about the many good, righteous people who thought of an idea, and this idea was focused around family and community life. These were religious, conscious people who understood their purpose in life and who knew, before writing their ideas down on paper, that they wanted to make sure they were pleasing to Allah.

When the first movie was produced in the 1800s, it was produced with respect to Allah and mankind. Many of these movies were focused on family life, values, and morals.

Before morals were thrown out the window, Allah's laws weren't even questioned. Nowadays, it's man's laws versus Allah's. These laws of man, when looked at closely, are based on deception, illusion, and wickedness in all forms and fashions.

Business itself is big, and it is crippling America to a point where Americans are blind to deception.

My mission is to guide humanity back to consciousness, to expose the deception that we are being blinded by and what I believe to be a solution for Americans. I believe righteous Muslims have an opportunity to save America, to put America's people back on the right track, to keep the dream from dying.

We must reevaluate our relationship with the Creator and expose the deceivers! We must work to put the universe back on the right course before Allah goes to war against us.

To better understand how sin became a trillion-dollar industry, I must first expose what many conscious people believe to be negative before I can show you the positive. If you don't understand the negative forces that we are up against, you will not be able to accept the positive forces without doubt.

This book will give you ideas, to help you establish a strong foundation, and to guide you to happiness while building a successful business. *It's all about business the lawful way.*

# Sin is a Trillion-Dollar Industry

I was born and raised in America in a time when Black Americans were fighting for their rights, and the 35thPresident was John F. Kennedy. I grew up in an era when Christian morals and values were well respected in America; even television programs were family-oriented.

When someone asks me, "Do you remember when you were a child?" I can only go back to age 3. I remember it like yesterday. I was sitting on the floor while my mother was watching a show on a little black-and-white television. I can remember my family watching Lassie, Shirley Temple, The Three Stooges Show, Casper, The Lone Ranger, The Twilight Zone, Perry Mason, Bonanza, I Love Lucy, Leave It To Beaver, and Mickey Mouse. During that time, Americans were big on making sure family programs were watched on television. It was always about a husband, his wife, and their children. Americans were big on family and marriage between a man and woman. The images that were predominantly shown on television were those of European Americans when I was growing up.

As a little girl, I didn't realize that discrimination was very strong in our country. It wasn't in the conversations around the family dinner table.

I grew up in a predominantly Black community; we were called Negroes then. Even when shame was brought to the family, it was kept sealed in a little black box somewhere inside your brain, and only the family knew the secrets inside that box. In other words, not even the community knew the troubles in your family. During that time, families watched out for others in our community; it was a close-knit community. My grandma used to say everyone knew everyone else's business because they had none of their own. But the truth is they knew when all the children misbehaved because that was all we knew. You didn't listen to grown-up conversations nor tend to adult business; you were always told to go to your bedroom even when your parents were in disagreement about something. Oh, how many of us glued our ears to the wall to hear what was going on until someone said, "I am telling Mama you're listening to their business." However, the point I am making is that certain things were kept hidden from us as children, including racism.

It was not until 3$^{rd}$ grade when my White teacher slapped me for telling a classmate to stop kicking me during a test. The teacher didn't want to hear any noises; on that day, a female classmate kicked me so hard I yelled out, "Stop kicking me!" The teacher snatched me up out of my chair, and she slapped me so hard that her handprint was seen on my face. She then threw me in a dark closet until lunchtime. This was the closest I got to experiencing discrimination—until I became a teenager.

Interestingly, as a young girl, I didn't fully understand discrimination the way our parents did, not until the day I was sitting in front of the television with my mom. I can remember us watching Martin Luther King's speech which was being broadcasted on the television. All of a sudden, my mother jumped straight up off the bed and started screaming. She ran out the front door screaming, "King is dead," over and over. This scared me; I had no idea what had just happened. This was the beginning of my family's discussions about discrimination. I was too young to understand what happened, though we stayed in our Black community. Though we lived near the border of DeKalb County, we were still fearful of going to DeKalb County because of the police; however, police brutality in the twenty-first century isn't anything like it was when I was growing up. You couldn't look in the face of a white cop—we saw them but didn't see them.

The majority of the jobs that Blacks had were labor jobs, cooking, cleaning, and nannying. Therefore, I believe the biggest sin in America then was the treatment of Blacks by so-called White Christians. If you want to talk about murdering innocent people; it is a known fact that millions of Blacks in America were killed only because of the color of their skin. We were always told to say, "Yes, sir" or "No, sir" to all adults, be they Black or White, but what was so incredible is that we heard Black adults say, "Yes (or no), sir (or ma'am)," to other White adults, but we never heard a White adult address Blacks in the same manner. We would hear Whites call nonwhites by their first names, or we would hear disrespectful Whites say "boy or gal," not even adding "Mr." or "Ms." to the names. Even with this, many Blacks held White American actors/actresses in high regard, their children were the roles models of Black American children, and their Jesus (PBUH) was our only "white hope"—even then we believed Jesus (PBUH) was White. Every good White person was the true American. We never saw naked women or men on television. White Americans took pride in protecting their children from anything that appeared to be distasteful; we didn't hear cursing on television, and everything was based on Christian values and morals even though Blacks were paraded around naked or half-naked. We could always find Blacks playing the role of maids, servants, butlers, cooks, servers, and drivers; they never would promote the family life (husband, wife, and children) of Blacks to other Whites, especially to their children. Every good character was a White person, and every bad character was a Black person. The Whites made sure they embedded this in the Negroes' heads and made it seem as if Blacks did not have an American family life. Remember what I said: "All the secrets were kept in a little black box somewhere in everyone's brain." We never saw any wrong done by White people; every bad thing that happened was shown on the news, and they would mention "a Black man killed," but if a White man or White woman committed a crime, we would never hear who it was. This is when Blacks start putting two and two together that the person must be White because the only time the color wasn't mentioned was when the person was White. Racism is America's biggest issue, and it is still in existence today.

Many White Americans live in Republican states, and some of the poorest people are Black; though you had many Whites who were also poor, the government takes care of them and their families through the welfare system that was actually set up for the soldiers' families when they were shipped out to war. However, when Black families needed the government to assist them, families were torn apart. One could only be on welfare if she were a single Black mother, and if she were caught with a man in her house, the government would take her children away from her, causing so many Black men to leave their families because they couldn't feed them, and the only thing to help the families was the welfare system. But for Whites, the husband could remain in the home. This is an unfair and unjust system that has destroyed so many Black families.

The question is, "What does sin have to do with racism?" Both brutality, committed against another human being, and oppression of a human being are sins; killing innocent men, women, and children is a sin.

Trafficking and enslaving human beings for free labor in any country is unlawful, and these sins have made this country millions of dollars.

# Halal Versus Haram Money

Do you know the difference between halal (lawful) and haram (unlawful) money? Lawful is everything that Allah has made permissible; therefore, believers are obedient and engage in halal things, which are pleasing to Allah. Haram (unlawful) pertains to prohibited things, which are displeasing to Allah, and things such as laws made to satisfy men's nafs (desires), which only please them and not Allah. Man makes things lawful, be it a marriage between homosexuals or illegal sex (fornication or adultery), even if they are forbidden by Allah.

In this chapter, you will be presented with stories from my deepest thoughts to help you visualize how profitable sin is and what is happening when we trade sin for peace, for our own body and soul.

The stories you are about to read are my own thoughts and/ or information I gathered in my research which allowed me to formulate a story for my readers to better understand the effect that sin has on one's life.

# Story 1

## The Food She Ate Altered My Life

I was created from a clot of congealed blood and a drop of sperm. I was in the womb of my mother for nine months nourished by nutrients that my mother consumed daily. The food that was supposed to help me develop into a healthy baby and grow to live a normal life—unfortunately, because my mother did not read the label—changed my life forever. My mother didn't know what kinds of ingredients were in the food that she bought. What she thought was 100% natural wasn't, and what she thought grew from crops didn't; she thought the animals were fed grass and grain but they weren't, and water that she thought was natural had ingredients in it. The prenatal vitamins that were supposed to protect me and help me grow didn't! Instead, I developed into a monster before I had a chance. I had a temper the day I was born; it was clear I wasn't ready. I just came out of my mother's womb when I felt a slap up against my butt; instead of crying, I turned my head to the left and looked at the doctor with clear hate and with a frown on my face. My parents thought I was adorable; my eyes were wide open. I was looking around at the colors in the room and the large faces that were staring at me. I couldn't speak, but I was able to notice who my parents were immediately. I recalled their voices were as clear to me as they are now from when I was in my mother's womb. I didn't understand what was happening, but I knew something was wrong. Am I a newborn or a model? The camera was flashing as I posed for every picture. *Wow*, I thought to myself, *what have they been feeding me?* Then I was ready to walk and talk. I lifted my head off the bed the first day. *Something is wrong*, I thought, and the only thing my parents kept saying was, "Wow, he is moving fast." Before they knew it, I had teeth growing out of my gums at two months; the doctor told my parents that it was normal: some babies are faster than others. However, my grandmother wasn't buying it—she knew something wasn't right. She told my parents I was growing faster than a normal baby should be growing, and my bones were so strong. I was ready to crawl at four months. My grandmother told my mother to take me to another doctor because it wasn't normal. My mother ignored her.

It was all because of money and shortcuts, and my mother soon discovered that the inexpensive meat and food that she bought and ate had double the dose of hormones in them, and most of the vegetables and meat she ate were genetically engineered. Also, the water that she drank was no longer water because it had certain ingredients in it. After time passed, my grandmother continued to pressure my parents to take me to another doctor, so finally they did. The doctor sat with my parents; now everything was wrong with me. Yes, they said I grew faster than a normal child should have; sadly they didn't know the effect it was going to have on me. Now I am an angry teenager, angry at the world not knowing why, and the only thing that was on my mind was killing and stealing. I came from a good family, so my mother couldn't understand what was happening. By the time I was fifteen I had been arrested ten times for theft, and by the time I was sixteen, I had been charged as an adult for murdering my father. No one could believe that I was sixteen. I stood 6'8" and weighed 250 pounds, with a full beard. When my mother came to court to hear my sentence, I was sad because she had no control over me anymore. I went from being her adorable little sweet baby boy to someone she didn't know. Then one day, I opened up a book, *"Sin Is A Trillion Dollar Industry"*. I realized I had been cheated of life, all because my mother didn't read the label on the food that she bought and because men found another way to make more money at the expense of human beings.

## FACTS

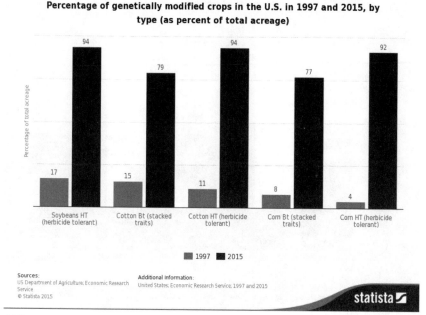

Percentage of genetically modified crops in the U.S. in 1997 and 2015, by type (as percent of total acreage)

- 1997
- 2015

Sources:
US Department of Agriculture; Economic Research Service
© Statista 2015

Additional Information:
United States; Economic Research Service; 1997 and 2015

statista

*"This statistic shows the proportion of crops that were genetically modified in the United States in 1997 and 2015, by type, as a percent of the total acreage of each crop. In 2014, some 91 percent of U.S. cotton crops were herbicide tolerant (HT cotton)."* (Statista)

Most people don't understand **genetically modified food**. It's important to understand what you are eating daily. According to USDA's Economic Research, Americans *eat nearly a ton of food a year*. If this is the case, America's government realized its growth and that it will be impossible to feed Americans at this consumption rate. Many farmers are dying off or forced into foreclosure. American families are not raising farmers' children; they are raising doctors, lawyers, teachers, and engineers. Since the end of slavery, many farmers couldn't maintain their lands, and many of their children went off to college. The government understood this, and something had to give, leaving scientists with no choice but to come up with a solution to feed Americans. A developer came up with a bright idea to modify food, to change the way food is grown. According to Wikipedia, the first genetically modified food that was introduced and sold to the American people was tomatoes in 1994.

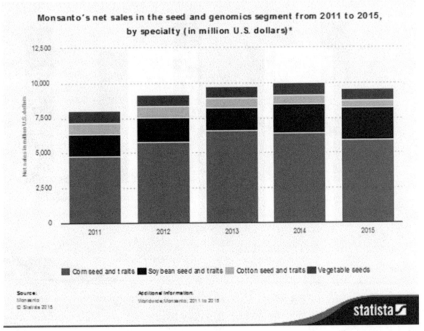

Monsanto's net sales in the seed and genomics segment from 2011 to 2015, by specialty (in million U.S. dollars)*

*"This statistic depicts agrochemical company Monsanto's net sales in the seed and genomics segment from 2011 to 2015, by specialty. In 2011, the corn seed and traits specialty came to approximately 4.81 billion U.S. dollars of net sales. Monsanto is an agricultural company specialized on genetic engineered seeds. The company is headquartered in St. Louis, Missouri."*

# Story 2

## If I Could Choose My Parents

Though I was conceived through fornication I was not given a choice, I was not able to choose my parents, well, I should say the woman and man who had illegal sex with no regard to my life, in their moment of sinful pleasures, didn't care if I lived or died . . .

Why should I care about her? Well, she did carry me for nine months. Maybe I should be grateful . . . but how could I be, when I couldn't make sense out of what she was feeding me? The only thing I could do is submit to something I had no control over—her intake of alcohol, drugs, and her relationship with men carrying STDs or HIV.

The prenatal care didn't even exist; the lack of nutrients was real. I didn't understand why she chose to have me instead of just aborting me.

Is she looking for love from me? How can I love her when she doesn't love herself? I was being tossed and turned, hit and kicked by the men having sex with her. I didn't even get to know the man whose sperm produced me. I had to experience all of this just for a one-night stand.

Where is this woman's *FAMILY*? Is there such a thing? I can't imagine my family not protecting me. The only shield I had to protect me is the shield God gave to me. This left me confused. "Oh dear God! Can I choose?"

I asked many questions, my whys went unanswered. Then my birth became my reality.

She screamed, and I was sad because I found myself happy knowing for a moment the pain she was feeling was because of me! If she only knew my screams went unheard, my kicks were ignored, and I was hurt from the pain that she inflicted on me and what she allowed others to do to me. My brain didn't have a chance. It was all deluded from the intake of cigarette smoke, drugs, and alcohol.

Then I heard . . .

"*Push*, push, push," the doctor said.

Then she screamed, "*TAKE IT OUT OF ME!! Take it out of me!*"

After all she put me through . . .

. . . I became an *"IT"*.

Now, I began to scream, "*NO, NO, NO,* dear God, please let me die!"

Only because I did not want to face the woman whom I will be calling my *mother* one day.

Now here I am with tremors from the abuse of alcohol and drugs, and instead of a mother caring for me and raising me, I have the government system.

# FACTS

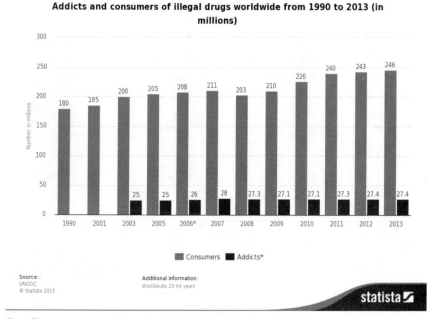

Addicts and consumers of illegal drugs worldwide from 1990 to 2013 (in millions)

*Source::*
UNODC
© Statista 2015

*Additional Information:*
Worldwide; 15-64 years

## Reading support

*This statistic shows the estimated number of addicts and consumers of illegal drugs worldwide from 1990 to 2013. In 1990, the number of consumers was estimated at some 180 million worldwide. Until 2010, this figure increased up to some 226 million.*

## Supplementary notes

*This statistic was assembled from several editions of the WDR. The source does not provide any information regarding the number of addicts before 2003.*

*\* The source calls them "problem drug users"; persons consuming illegal drugs on a regular basis.*

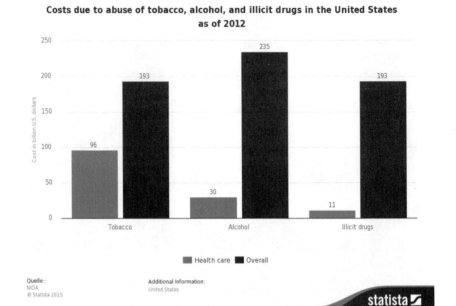

**Costs due to abuse of tobacco, alcohol, and illicit drugs in the United States as of 2012**

Quelle::
NIDA
© Statista 2015

Additional Information:
United States

statista

### Reading support

*This statistic shows costs related to the abuse of tobacco, alcohol, and illicit drugs in the United States as of 2012. In the U.S., the abuse of tobacco, alcohol, and illicit drugs resulted in costs of over 600 billion U.S. dollars annually related to crime, lost work productivity and healthcare.*

According to Turbo Tax, the federal excise on cigarettes grossed $8,512,263,000 in tax revenue for 2009. For alcohol, the figure is $5,626,187, 000.

Every day, children are born to parents who use legal drugs during pregnancy. The two most used legal drugs are alcohol and tobacco. Did you know, according to the World Health Organization (WHO), that *"tobacco is deadly in any form or disguise"*? Also, *tobacco kills nearly 6 million people each year, of which more than 600,000 are nonsmokers dying from breathing secondhand smoke." (http://www. who.int/tobacco/wntd/en/)*

In Islam, suicide is forbidden, and if we take a closer look at cigarettes, it is a known fact that cigarettes cause major health issues such as lung cancer, throat cancer, and, in most cases, heart failure and other diseases. Therefore, smokers are slowly killing themselves, which is forbidden.

Did you know that alcohol was illegal in the United States Constitution? It was banned in the United States until 1933. Man legalized what was forbidden by Allah, though before Allah forbade drinking alcohol, it was abrogated in the Quran; it was legal and then forbidden. Even in America, it was a known fact that morals were high, and the government didn't want to legalize a substance that most likely will cause disorderly behavior. With this being said, alcohol, just like any other substance that has been legalized, has caused fetal alcohol syndrome, babies to be born prematurely and/or born as an addict and even increased risks for SIDS (sudden infant death syndrome). To learn more or to talk to someone you know who may not know about the effect that drugs have on their unborn child, please visit http://superiorhealthfoundation.org/drug-addicted-baby-awareness.

# Story 3

## Born?

I didn't ask to be born in a world of confusion, but I was taught that we all are children of Adam and Eve. I was told that the woman that birthed me had no interest in me. She was paid to carry me for nine months, and after she birthed me, I was handed over to my parents. I can remember during first grade I was in a Christmas play, which my parents attended. I noticed that the parents of my friends weren't like mine. My parents were both male, and my friend's parents were male and female. My friends used to ask me, "Is that your daddy and your uncle?" My answer was, "No, they are my parents." Then they would say, "Oh, your dad and your stepdad?" What I thought was normal wasn't; it was normal to have stepparents. What I didn't know is that my parents were homosexual. I learned about homosexuality in sixth grade. I loved them both, and they were the best parents ever. I have the utmost respect for the men who were my "parents"; it got even harder for me when I got older and began to recognize the difference, and I felt it was wrong for people to choose a lifestyle without the consent of children. I do understand young children have little choices; this is where laws should protect children. When I saw the two men who raised me kiss, and when I mistakenly walked in on them having intercourse, it did something to my heart. I got very sick to my stomach, the thought of seeing the two men that I loved as my "parents" made me question myself. Nothing about that seems right. I loved them because they raised me, but I hated them because I felt like I didn't belong, though I had the best out of life, lived in the best of houses and neighborhoods, they dressed me very well, and they bought me anything I wanted. I felt like they were buying my love and expecting me to accept their lifestyle. I was very clear that I had desires for girls and not boys. Unfortunately, having two gay parents left psychological marks; for example, I didn't want to play contact sports with boys, and I didn't want to hang out only with boys because I didn't want to be looked at like my "parents."

I had to live with it and be laughed at or be talked about as "the little boy with gay parents." I always defended my parents, and the ugly part is that I grew up ashamed of the lifestyle that was chosen for me. When company came over, it was always same-sex couples with their children. There was a lot of damage done, and on top of it all, they did not understand. I often wonder whether gay couples would have children if they had their own city. If not, eventually they would die, and no one would be left in that city without a woman carrying a man's sperm. I asked myself, if this is the case, why didn't God let men give birth or allow women to get pregnant by another woman. I realized this wasn't something Allah made lawful; this is something man made lawful. But when I debate with my parents about this, they brush it off as if I don't understand.

I brought my girlfriend over to my house one day. I warned her prior to meeting my parents that they were a male couple, and that I was conceived by some unknown man and woman out there, and it was clear that I had more of my father's hormones than my mother's. I have no desire for another man. Maybe the parents who bought me were hoping that by raising me in a same-sex household I would accept their homosexuality.

My parents were excited about me having company, and so was my girlfriend. She wanted to meet them. They were very surprised that I brought her over and that I told her that they were my parents. I felt they were confused with their gender. My date wasn't uncomfortable because her parents were both women. See, we were determined to break a cycle that we were forced into and were forced to accept. A lifestyle that didn't seem to be natural to us; we knew we were different, and we accepted that even though the parents who were raising us didn't accept the fact that we didn't want gay parents. We did want a normal life, and we didn't like being in a world where the majority of the men and women were attracted to the opposite sex instead of the same sex, and we had parents who were the same sex. We didn't like the fact that couples who adopted us didn't understand that we didn't like being different and being abused or mistreated because of our "parents." I am clear that Allah created women to carry a fetus, that it takes a male's sperm and a woman's egg to create a baby, and that Allah did not make man to be pregnant by another man or a woman to get pregnant by another woman. Isn't it the natural way of life? Isn't it a reason for a union to be between a man and a woman? It is called reproduction. The point I am making is that I am not fighting your right to love who you love or to marry who you want to marry; I am fighting for the right of children to choose who they want to be raised by. We children have to live in this world of confusion; don't make us hate before we have the chance to love, and don't make us choose because you chose for us. Some of us are already born to men and women who had no intentions of raising us. Isn't that enough? But to have men adopt us with the intention of raising us as if they gave birth to us without realizing the effect it will have on us? Yes, you were great parents, but my life was filled with hate and anger in this world of confusion.

Before religion, Allah created man and then He created a woman to be his mate. For the sake of argument, we can say this is a known fact.

## FACTS

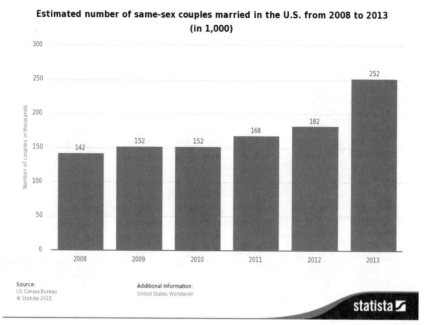

**Estimated number of same-sex couples married in the U.S. from 2008 to 2013 (in 1,000)**

Source:
US Census Bureau
© Statista 2015

Additional Information:
United States; Worldwide

statista

Reading support

*This statistic displays the estimated number of same-sex couples that are married in the United States from 2008 to 2013. In 2012, there was an estimated 182,000 couples in the country. After the defeat of the Defense of Marriage Act (DOMA), the number of marriages increased rapidly.*

According to the Gay Law Report, *"65,000 children live with same-sex parents reported in 2000 Census. In 2012, 110,000 live with gay parents."*

According to Forbes, "We estimate that if the laws were changed, gay couples currently living together would collectively spend $16.8 billion to get hitched."

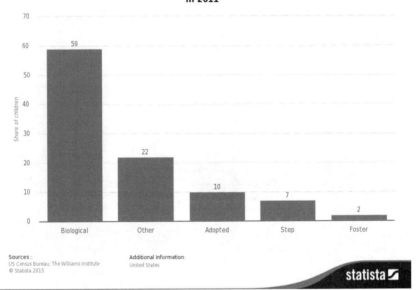

Same-sex couple households in the U.S.: Relationship of children and parents in 2011

*Reading support*

This statistic shows the kind of relationship American children that are growing up in same-sex households have with their parents as of 2011. That year, 59 percent of children living in same-sex households were identified as the biological children of the householder.

# Story 4

## Your War!

Gun shots . . . bang, bang, bang . . . bomb drops from the sky . . . boom, boom, boom . . . as we run for our dear lives, crossing streets, hiding under bridges, swimming in lakes filled with blood. Whose war is this? I am innocent. I hid behind an empty building with my parents and some other unknown men, women, and children while what I thought was rain dropping from the sky was blood dripping from my father's head. A bullet grazed his head, which left a wound; my mother wrapped it with her scarf, but it bled terribly. "Run!!" my father said. I turned around to the crowd of people behind the wall, and I watched them drop one by one. I saw my father and mother fall to the ground too; my mother fell to the ground in my father's arm. The next thing I knew was someone grabbing me, and we both fell into a hole. I landed on top of a dead man. I heard feet above the earth as they ran, the noises from guns being fired, and then I heard a yell, and all of a sudden it got quiet. I was no longer afraid because the dead man who held me close with his hand gripped around my wrist was the guardian angel that saved me. I waited until nightfall, and then I climbed out of the hole that was deep enough to hold at least ten more bodies. I reached the top of the hole, and there I saw my parents and my sister both shot dead like animals in the streets. I pulled each one of them to the manhole, I pushed them in, and I said a prayer. "If there is a God above, let them rest in peace and may we meet again in heaven where there is peace." I covered the hole with all the dirt I could see. I wanted to bury the others but I couldn't. I began to travel in the dark following the moon and the stars. Tears fell from my eyes while I cried in grief. "Whose war is this for?" I yelled and yelled. "We are innocent men, women, and children. This is your war and your turn is coming. It's just a matter of time. You will be defeated and your men, women, and children will be shot down in the streets like dogs. Watch and see. This is your war, not our war, and you killed innocent people like dogs in the street!"

## FACTS

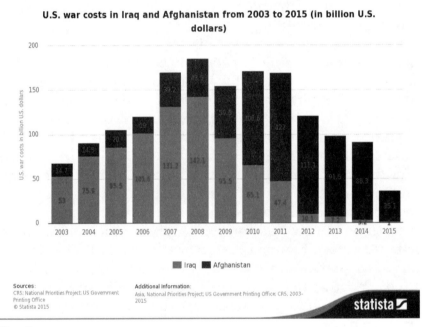

**U.S. war costs in Iraq and Afghanistan from 2003 to 2015 (in billion U.S. dollars)**

■ Iraq  ■ Afghanistan

Sources:
CRS: National Priorities Project; US Government Printing Office
© Statista 2015

Additional Information:
Asia, National Priorities Project; US Government Printing Office; CRS, 2003-2015

**statista**

*Reading support*

*The statistic shows the cost of the war in Iraq and in Afghanistan from 2003 to 2015. In 2013, the costs of the war in Afghanistan amounted to 91.5 billion U.S. dollars.*

According to the Watson Institute, International and Public Affairs, Brown University, approximately 210,000 Afghan, Iraqi, and Pakistani civilians have died violent deaths as a direct result of the wars. And over 6,800 US service members and over 6,900 contractors have died in the wars in Iraq and Afghanistan.

The Bush administration, which started the war in Iraq, asked Congress to approve $196 billion to pay for the wars in Iraq and Afghanistan, according to the *New York Times*.

# Story 5

## Breathe

I gave birth to a seven-pound baby girl. She was born January 9, 1970. I remember it like it was yesterday, my firstborn. My husband came home that evening and I was standing in the kitchen making his dinner when my water sac broke. "Honey!" I yelled out, and he came running to the kitchen. "It's time." He was so nervous that he ran out the door screaming, "It's time." I walked to the room to get my suitcase, which I'd packed ahead of time for this day. I called the hospital operator. "I am nine months pregnant. My water sack broke. Please send an ambulance." I gave my address, and in twenty minutes, the paramedics were at our home. When I got to the hospital, I started contracting. The nurse put me on the monitor; she couldn't get a good reading on my baby. They rushed me to surgery; I had to have a C-section. When they pulled the baby out of me, I heard the doctor say, "Breathe, little one, breathe." I was scared. I began to cry, yelling, "Please, God, don't let her die. Breathe." I said it over and over, then I heard a cough. Immediately they put her on oxygen. Angel, I called her. My husband was summoned into the room. They explained that my baby was having difficulty breathing. We asked, "Why?" Then my doctor asked, "How many cigarettes did you smoke a day?" I hesitated then I said immediately, "Not that many." The doctor asked again, "How many is 'not that many'?" I told him that I smoked a pack a day. My husband said, "We both smoked a pack a day." The doctor explained that the nicotine affected our baby; she was having difficulty breathing.

"Breathe, baby Angel. Breathe, baby Angel." She lived for three weeks and three days. Her lungs were diseased. Every pack of cigarettes that I bought had a warning label on it, a warning for pregnant women that I totally ignored. For nine months, I smoked a pack a day, 252 packs total. Nine months of carrying her wasn't worth her not being able to breathe. Now I am burying my baby whom I caused to die only because I ignored the label's warning signs. I am sorry, my little Angel!

## FACTS

The Surgeon General stated that cigarettes could cause babies to be premature or have low birth weight.

***"Smoking leads to disease and disability and harms nearly every organ of the body.***

- *More than 16 million Americans are living with a disease caused by smoking.*
  **Smoking is the leading cause of preventable death.**
- *Worldwide, tobacco use causes nearly 6 million deaths per year, and current trends show that tobacco use will cause more than 8 million deaths annually by 2030.[2]*
- *Cigarette smoking is responsible for more than 480,000 deaths per year in the United States, including an estimated 41,000 deaths resulting from secondhand smoke exposure. This is about one in five deaths annually, or 1,300 deaths every day.[1]*
- *On average, smokers die 10 years earlier than nonsmokers.[3]*
- *If smoking continues at the current rate among U.S. youth, 5.6 million of today's Americans younger than 18 years of age are expected to die prematurely from a smoking-related illness. The tobacco industry spends billions of dollars each year on cigarette advertising and promotions.[4]*
- *In 2012, $9.17 billion was spent on advertising and promotion of cigarettes—more than $25 million every day, or more than $1 million every hour.*

Report from CDC (Centers for Disease Control and Prevention)

# Story 6

## Hospitals vs. Prisons

John Vaxim, CEO of "keep them ill and in the hospital" versus Mark Vaxim, CEO of "put them in prison." Hospitals are needed and prisons/jails are needed. John thought about having a hospital for years until he became the CEO of one. His hospital was having financial difficulties until the hospital built a research center on the west wing. John needed people to participate in experimental drugs. John came up with a bright idea: seek the men from the prison that Mark owned throughout America. "Mark, I need you to let your prisoners try this experimental drug, but first, the men must first be injected with a virus, then we will then have them take the experimental drug." Mark agreed to test one hundred men; Mark utilized the men who had twenty years to life without a possibility of parole. John set it up where each prisoner would receive this virus. Instead of telling the prisoners that it was a virus, they told them it was a vaccine to keep them from catching the virus. Each prisoner fell ill, and each prisoner had to go back to the hospital to be put on this experimental drug that was supposed to make them feel better. Out of the 100 prisoners who got the virus, 60 died and 40 lived. The forty who lived had strong immune systems. John apologized to Mark for his prisoners' deaths, but Mark didn't care—he made $1,000 per prisoner. Mark asked John to tell him when he needed more prisoners to help him perfect the drug. John said, "Hospitals and prisons are big business . . . I'll keep them sick and you'll keep them in prison."

# FACTS

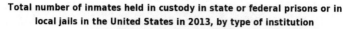

**Total number of inmates held in custody in state or federal prisons or in local jails in the United States in 2013, by type of institution**

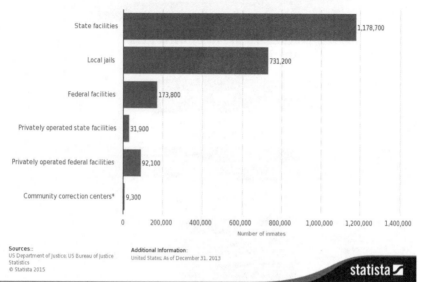

Sources::
US Department of Justice; US Bureau of Justice Statistics
© Statista 2015

Additional Information:
United States; As of December 31, 2013

statista

*Reading support*

*This statistic shows the total number of inmates held in custody in state or federal prisons or in local jails in the United States in 2013, by type of institution. In 2013, about 31,900 federal prisoners were held in privately operated facilities.*

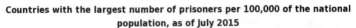

**Countries with the largest number of prisoners per 100,000 of the national population, as of July 2015**

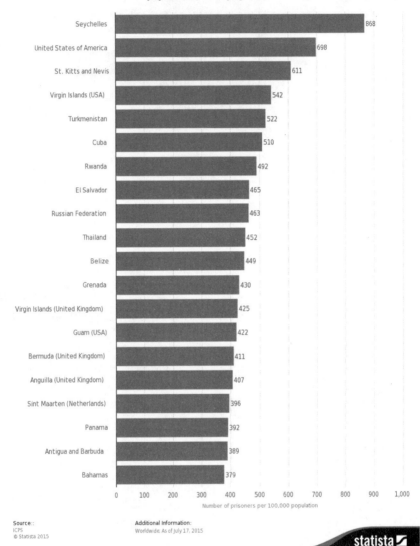

| | |
|---|---|
| Seychelles | 868 |
| United States of America | 698 |
| St. Kitts and Nevis | 611 |
| Virgin Islands (USA) | 542 |
| Turkmenistan | 522 |
| Cuba | 510 |
| Rwanda | 492 |
| El Salvador | 465 |
| Russian Federation | 463 |
| Thailand | 452 |
| Belize | 449 |
| Grenada | 430 |
| Virgin Islands (United Kingdom) | 425 |
| Guam (USA) | 422 |
| Bermuda (United Kingdom) | 411 |
| Anguilla (United Kingdom) | 407 |
| Sint Maarten (Netherlands) | 396 |
| Panama | 392 |
| Antigua and Barbuda | 389 |
| Bahamas | 379 |

Number of prisoners per 100,000 population

Source::
ICPS
© Statista 2015

Additional Information:
Worldwide; As of July 17, 2015

statista ◢

## Prisoners in the United States

*As the statistic above illustrates, the United States has one of the highest rates of incarceration in the world. With 698 inmates per 100 thousand of population, the U.S. is by far the leader among industrialized nations in incarceration. Russia comes closest at 463, though there is no data regarding China's incarceration rate available.*

*Not only is the U.S. among the leading countries worldwide in incarcerations per 100 thousand of population, but it was also home to the largest total number of prisoners in 2014.*

*Roughly 2.2 million people were incarcerated in the United States in 2014. China's estimated prison population totaled to 1.7 million people that year. Other nations with population sizes comparable to the United States have far fewer prisoners.*

It is an issue when prisoners who are housed in America outnumber an entire population in another country.

According to Global Research:

*There are approximately 2 million inmates in state, federal and private prisons throughout the country. According to California Prison Focus,"no other society in human history has imprisoned so many of its own citizens." The figures show that the United States has locked up more people than any other country: a half million more than China, which has a population five times greater than the U.S.*

*Statistics reveal that the United States holds 25% of the world's prison population, but only 5% of the world's people. From less than 300,000 inmates in 1972, the jail population grew to 2 million by the year 2000.*

*The prison industry complex is one of the fastest-growing industries in the United States and its investors are on Wall Street. "This multi-million-dollar industry has its own trade exhibitions, conventions, websites, and mail-order/ Internet catalogs. It also has direct advertising campaigns, architecture companies, construction companies, investment houses on Wall Street, plumbing supply companies, food supply companies, armed security, and padded cells in a large variety of colors."*

*Who is investing? At least 37 states have legalized the contracting of prison labor by private corporations that* *mount their operations inside state prisons. The list of such companies contains the cream of U.S. corporate society: IBM, Boeing, Motorola, Microsoft, AT&T, Wireless, Texas Instrument, Dell, Compaq, Honeywell, Hewlett-Packard, Nortel, Lucent Technologies, 3Com, Intel, Northern Telecom, TWA, Nordstrom's, Revlon, Macy's, Pierre Cardin, Target Stores, and many more. All of these businesses are excited about the economic boom generated by prison labor. Just between 1980 and 1994, profits went up from $392 million to $1.31 billion.*

*From Global Research (http://www.globalresearch.ca/the-prison-industry-in-the-united-states-big-business-or-a-new-form-of-slavery/8289)*

In my opinion, this is one of the reasons many Americans are not employed.

# Story 7

## Gambling

I can remember the meals on our dinner table like yesterday. We went from having meals three times a day, seven days a week, to once a day. My mother lost her job and my dad did too. By the time my mother got on welfare, she owed so many people that the food stamps we thought we could depend on became useless because my mother and father paid people back with the food stamps. Sometimes, we barely had that one meal a day. We dared to complain; my brothers and sisters went to bed hungry most nights, and we couldn't wait to get to school just to eat breakfast and lunch. The school began to replace the meals that were missing from our table at home. Every day my parents hoped to win the lottery, and they sold us dreams every day. Their favorite dream line was *"WHEN WE GET RICH, when we get rich."* They were gambling our food off our table and the clothes off our backs. Soon it would be our home. My dad pawned the television and his guns, and each time they would buy another lottery ticket hoping they would win their way out of their sinful acts. It didn't matter whether they won or lost; every dime they won they would use to buy more tickets hoping to win more. It was greed indeed. The lights got turned off, then the gas was shut off, and then we were getting ready to be evicted. We didn't know whether to pray to God to let our parents win or cry ourselves to sleep. Gambling their lives away on the *"WHEN WE GET RICH, when we get rich"* dream, while my siblings and I were dreaming of food on the table, lights, gas, and clothes on our backs, only to be disappointed again.

One day, my dad jumped up. "We won Cash 3," my dad yelled. We jumped too, happy that we were going to eat more than just peanut butter on white bread without jelly. "Yes, yes," my brothers screamed out, "Dad, can we go to McDonald's?" My dad said, "Nope!" Instead, my dad went to the store and returned with another loaf of white bread and peanut butter. He looked over at my mother. "If we win this time, I will buy groceries," he said with a smirk on his face. My oldest brother walked out of the house mumbling, "Are they for real?" Gambling was destroying my entire family, all of this just to be broke over and over again and nothing to show for it but being broke. Numbers, numbers, and more numbers. Dad lost every cent that night. No more money to gamble with. We lost our parents to gambling. The last thing I remember about my parents before my grandmother adopted us was the day they dropped us off at my grandmother's house. My mom said, "Your father and I got a job out of town. We will be back when we can." We never saw them again; we don't know what happened to them. No phone calls, no holidays, nothing—just broken promises.

## FACTS

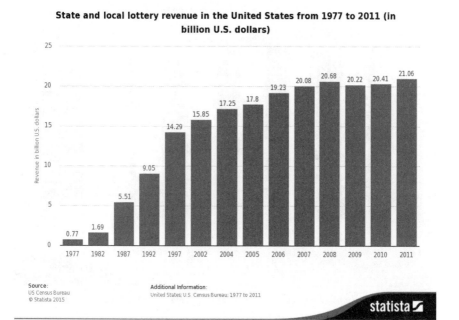

State and local lottery revenue in the United States from 1977 to 2011 (in billion U.S. dollars)

*Reading support*

*The statistic shows the state and local lottery revenue in the United States from 1977 to 2011. In 2011, state and local government collected about 21.1 billion U.S. dollars by lottery.*

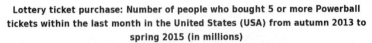

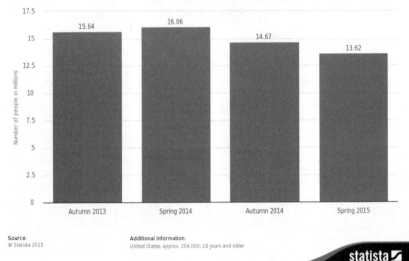

*This statistic illustrates the number of people who bought 5 or more Powerball tickets in the United States (USA) from autumn 2013 to spring 2015. In spring 2014, the number of people in the U.S. who bought 5 or more Powerball tickets within the last month amounted to 16.06 million.*

According to the *New York Times* in 1999, *"More than five million Americans are pathological or problem gamblers, and another 15 million are at risk of falling into the same morass, according to a study reported last month by the National Gambling Impact Study Commission, a nine-member Federal panel. More than 5 percent of people develop a gambling problem at some time, twice the rate of cocaine addiction, said Dr. Nancy Petry, a psychologist studying treatment for compulsive gamblers at the University of Connecticut Health Center in Farmington."*

According to the American Gaming Association, *"Gaming is a powerful economic engine that contributes $240 billion to the nation's economy and generates $38 billion in tax revenues that pay for critical public services. 1. The industry also supports 1.7 million jobs and nearly $74 billion in income* *for these workers and their families. 2 While most Americans are familiar with the traditional types of jobs held by the front-line employees who provide world-class service to tens of millions of customers every year, the diversity of jobs gaming supports extends far beyond the casino floor. For the first time, a new report by Oxford Economics examines the quality, range and skills associated with the more than 200 types of jobs at hundreds of casinos across 40 states."*

*"The gambling industry around the world is huge, but the biggest market is the United States, where gamblers lost a staggering $119 billion in 2013."*

*Reported by The Week (http://theweek.com/articles/451623/ how-did-americans-manage-lose-119-billion-gambling- last-year)*

According to CNN Money, *"Last year Americans spent a total of $70.15 billion on lottery tickets, according to the North American Association of State and Provincial Lotteries."*

*"SIN IS A TRILLION-DOLLAR INDUSTRY"* and all the ills of this society lead to self-destruction; even if you feel you have won, you still lose!

# Story 8

## Follow the Money Trail

*"Oh, say! Can you see by the dawn's early light,*
*What so proudly we hailed at the twilight's last gleaming,*
*Whose broad stripes and bright stars, through the perilous fight,*
*O'er the ramparts we watched were so gallantly streaming,*
*And the rocket's red glare, the bombs bursting in air,*
*Gave proof through the night that our flag was still there*
*Oh, say! Does that star spangled banner yet wave,*
*O'er the land of the free and the home of the brave."*

*"I pledge allegiance to the Flag of the United States and to*
*the Republic for which it stands; one Nation indivisible with*
*liberty and justice for all."*

America, America, America, the land of the Natives, the land
with beautiful green pasture and fresh water for drinking
and bathing. Now here comes Christopher Columbus, who
sailed all the way from Europe in the middle of the night—
yes, they were so proud to discover a land that was already
discovered, a land that had human beings on it, who spoke
a different language, a people who lived comfortably with
the means provided by God above. Everything was pure,
there were little to no diseases, and growth was abundant
with no name on its soil. "Was it America?" Columbus went
back to his country to tell the men what he found and the
desire to move swiftly to take the land from the Natives.
Columbus's crew rode up to the Natives like a thief in
the middle of the night, making promises after promises
filled with lies and deceit. The Englishmen introduced the

Natives to their filth—swine, alcohol, and guns—until they gained the Natives' trust. The Europeans became the Natives' nightmare; Columbus and his men deceived the Natives, then the killing began, starting with the men. The women and elderly men were enslaved. Now comes the celebration . . . on this day, we will call it "Thanksgiving" in America. Most European countries took a piece of the land throughout America until it became the North, South, East, and West. Each region had their own leaders, and each leader had their own personality which influenced the weak-minded people. Greed made them fight one another. Destruction began throughout America, and this caused regulations to kick in; agreements and treaties were developed between the North and the South. Then the Englishmen got tired of enslaving their own kind. One leader said, "We must start a war so we can capture us some slaves. We will not enslave our kind anymore and the few Natives we have left we will set them free. Too many of our men have begun to marry the Natives and they have bore our children." One of the leaders asked, "Where will we get slaves to work our land?" His sentiments echoed throughout America. "It's time to visit Africa." So they sailed out to Africa with their "fake promises." Once they arrived, they introduced Africa's leaders to the same poison they introduced to the Native Americans. These evildoers came with their little silver and gold to trade, as well as weapons and their clothes, until they tricked and cheated the African people out of everything, killing many of their men, capturing majority of them, along with their women and children. They returned to America with ships loaded with Africans. "Hear ye, hear ye, the slaves have arrived. We will sell them off one by one to the highest bidder."

America, America, America, the land of the murderers, who confessed that they were Christians while they were unjust to many of their slaves, breaking their backs, stripping them from their families, hanging them from trees while every European-born child watched and learned how to kill, beat, and hang a human being. "Hear ye, hear ye, if any European male sleeps with a Negro slave and that slave gives birth to a child, you must sell that child as a slave or kill that child. Any child with even one drop of black blood in it is still a 'Negro.'" America got its glory for being the best negotiator, manipulator, deceiver, cheater, and liar. America kept tricking people into treaties with broken promises, and those who rejected their promises would be bullied with threats or war and have their lands destroyed until they submitted.

Then came another generation that wasn't like the generation of their parents, a generation that didn't see color, a generation that felt all people were equal. This new generation was different from their slave master parents; they were thinkers and readers. This generation consisted of children of "slave masters" and "European children," but you still had a majority that were determined not to let these slaves free unless they were killed. There was so much bloodshed on America's soil. Then it happened: Africans became free. Some didn't want to be free, and then you had Negro children who were mixed because they had white blood in them, and if they weren't white enough, they were disowned. Some were children of the Natives, but the majority were European. They refused to allow "Negroes" to be successful, so they set out to build relationships with every race other than Africans.

Paying Chinese people 5 cents per handbag and clothes— no worries; since our slaves want to be free, we will make sure not one of them has a job or benefits from European people. We would allow Chinese people to move to America to supply us with technology and goods and services. Then the Europeans went to Spain—no worries; we will allow your people to move to America, but they must take over the jobs that the slaves used to do. We don't want the Negroes in our houses, going to our schools with our children, or teaching our children. We will give Spanish women hotel jobs. They can be our maids, and their men can maintain our lawns and work on our houses. We must drive these Negroes off our land. No worries, we will pay Spanish people 50 cents for their labor. Europeans tried to break Negroes in hopes of pushing them off their stolen land; they did everything to destroy Negroes. They tried to kill them off, but instead they were able to get Negroes to turn on each other with tricks, lies, and broken promises, then when they couldn't kill them off fast enough, they noticed with every death a child was born, producing more and more babies. Then they worked hard at intoxicating their minds with drugs, alcohol, and cigarettes so the Negroes couldn't think.

The witch-hunt has begun! America, America, America, the thieves have destroyed you, the murderers have destroyed you, and the liars have destroyed you, all because of greed. Now the American people are fighting to repair you before it is too late?

America sold out their own people, gave up their own country for another people to develop it and run it, and now, many of their beauty queens and kings have died, leaving no heirs behind who shared their same ideology and values. The little mixed babies they made slaves of or killed off, leaving no one to continue their legacy. America, America, America was terrorizing people on their own land, stripping people from their families and destroying everything in their path. Once freedom came to a people by their own laws, Americans fought so hard to kill off the Negro race only because they feared their men and women would marry the Negroes. Forget that "master" was sneaking out sleeping with Negro gals.

America, America, America is no longer America. It died the day the Natives were killed. As years passed, all the Europeans did to America is haunting them now. Is it too late to repair America? Now Americans are fighting to take back their jobs, and their country, only because America didn't like a people (Negroes) that God created.

## FACTS

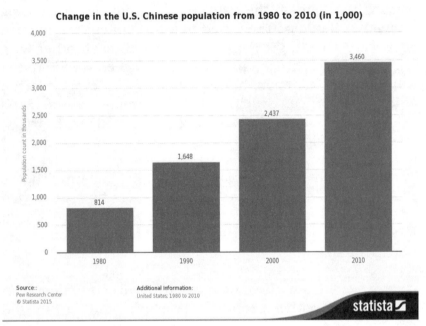

Change in the U.S. Chinese population from 1980 to 2010 (in 1,000)

Source::
Pew Research Center
© Statista 2015

Additional Information:
United States; 1980 to 2010

statista

*Reading support*

*This statistic shows the change in the United States' Chinese population from 1980 to 2010. In 1980, there were 814,000 Chinese-Americans (Chinese immigrants and people with Chinese heritage) living in the United States.*

**Hispanic population groups in the United States, by country of origin 2010 (In 1,000)**

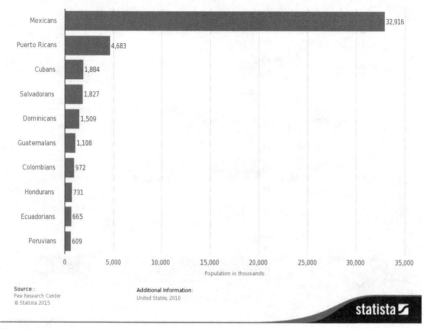

Source::
Pew Research Center
© Statista 2015

Additional Information:
United States, 2010

statista

*Reading support*

*This statistic depicts the 10 largest groups of people with Hispanic origin living in the United States as of 2010. At this time 32,916,000 people of Mexican descent were living in the United States.*

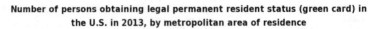

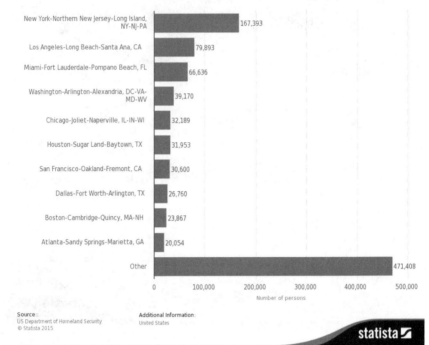

*Reading support*

*This graph shows the number of persons obtaining legal permanent resident status in the United States in 2013, by metropolitan area of residence. In 2013, about 167,393 persons living in the New York-Northern New Jersey-Long Island metropolitan area received a green card.*

According to PBS
(http://www.pbs.org/wgbh/aia/part4/4p2957.html):

*To the fugitive slave fleeing a life of bondage, the North was a land of freedom. Or so he or she thought. Upon arriving there, the fugitive found that, though they were no longer slaves, neither were they free. African Americans in the North lived in a strange state of semi-freedom. The North may have had emancipated its slaves, but it was not ready to treat the blacks as citizens . . . nor sometimes even as human beings.*

To see foreign trade reported by United States Census Bureau   http://www.census.gov/foreign-trade/balance/c5700.html

According to U.S. News (http://www.usnews.com/news/blogs/data-mine/2014/12/11/outsourcing-to-china-cost-us-32-million-jobs-since-2001):

*Between 2001 and 2013, the expanded trade deficit with China cost the U.S. 3.2 million jobs, and three quarters of those jobs were in manufacturing, according to the Economic Policy Institute, a left-leaning Washington think tank. Those manufacturing jobs lost accounted for about two-thirds of all jobs lost within the industry over the 2001 to 2013 period.*

There seemed to be a bright future for immigrants who came to work for Europeans for low wages versus freed slaves with no wages. Many Europeans didn't like the idea, and many of their children weren't comfortable with non-English speaking people working and living within their walls. As time passed, many Europeans moved to other countries or to their native land, leaving many behind who were born in America to clean up the mess caused by them not liking a certain race. In my opinion, because of their own hate, many dark-skinned non-Americans dislike being identified as black though they were black, just not Americans. This attitude caused many divisions among people of color to a point that blacks became hated all over the world by so many people and unlawfully mistreated and cheated out of life . . . but of course, human trafficking is big business.

# Story 9

## Media is Destroying America: Is it by Design?

I was sitting at my desk early Saturday morning when I got a memo to do a story on Sharia Law, and at the end of the memo, it said "stir up the naïve people." Being a new reporter for this said company (without mentioning the company's name), I was sad because the laws of God are there in all the Books, and because I am Jewish, it was hard for me to portray Islamic Law to be something other than the Laws of God. If I had to discuss the laws of Judaism from the Torah or the Laws of God from the Christian Bible, then naïve people would be outraged for exposing the Laws of God from their own Books. If we, the Jewish, had forced laws on the "naïve people," maybe America would be a better place, and immoral behavior would be in question.

"Stir up the naïve people." It is believed that many non-Jewish Americans who are Christians are so vulnerable to a point that all we have to do is put it on the news, be it truth, falsehood, or a mix of both. I remember my father being one of the owners of a news station, and it was him who encouraged me to go into journalism.

I can remember when we sat around the dinner table one night, and I asked my father a question. "Why not just tell the American people the truth?" My father looked at me straight in my eyes, a look that I had never seen before. Then he said, "The truth. What is the truth? American people prefer to believe a lie instead of truth!" Then Sally, our Negro American maid walked into the room while saying, "Amen." I turned to her and said, "You prefer believing a lie rather than the truth"? She said, "No, sir, I prefer to believe the truth than a lie, but Negroes are put in positions to only lie than to tell the truth just to stay alive." Then my father turned to me and said that the Nazis made us tell lies just to stay alive and some white Americans were just as bad as Nazis. Their entire lives were built on lies. They killed millions of African slaves, raped their women slaves, castrated male slaves, hung innocent men, women, and children from trees, had their dogs attack and, in some cases, eat the slaves. When my parents arrived in America, little by little we started buying everything. Many American whites sold their own people out; many of them were slaves themselves until they changed from enslaving their own people to enslaving Negroes from Africa. Then many Jews decided to shift and start hiring Negroes to work for Jewish businesses, refusing to do business with many white American Christians who didn't like us in the early days. We found more hypocrisy in their faith, in their churches, and they used religion to hate us for not believing that Jesus (pbuh) came to earth.

We may be small in number in America but we are large according to our pockets. We bought everything we could buy, and most importantly, we monopolized Americans' pastime (entertainment). Americans spent more money on entertainment than on developing strong citizens in the areas of science, math, and religion. We used what their forefathers used to steer them up—their religion. The truth is we used America to help us take land from Palestinian people. We used Americans to turn on their own people; we knew it was easy for them to turn on their own religion. We were able to succeed by using the media to put fear in American people's hearts; we used the same scare tactics that the American whites used on Negroes only because they did not want Negroes to prosper in their states. The news spread like wildfire: "American people must kill every slave before they kill your people, rape your children, and murder your men. These Negroes are filthy animals. God made them slaves to us, and now they are free because of Abraham Lincoln who sold us out." Now we are using their scare tactics to make them believe that if we allow Muslims to live in our country the way we allowed Negroes, that they will take over and utilize the Sharia Law to destroy America. Naïve people believe everything without investigating. All it takes is to reach those "white supremacists" who hate Negroes, Jews, gays, and immigrants to a point where they will lump all of them together in one boat. But to get this to work, we have to bring in a few people to steer up the naïve Americans by reminding them of 9/11/2001. What many American people do not know is that majority of Jews name their children after their prophets, and some Muslims give their children the same names, such as Isa (Jesus) and Ibrahim (Abraham). It's easy to say a Muslim did the crime on 9/11. Many whites framed blacks for years to scare Americans, starting with their own government—how they planted people to start wars among themselves, utilizing lies, because they knew that people prefer to believe a lie than the truth, and they will not investigate the facts. What many American people do not know is that we all use the Arabic term "Allah" in the Middle East before Prophet Muhammad (pbuh) came, because Allah only means "God." When we say "Allah," we're not talking about gods other than the God of Abraham, Moses, Isaac, and Jesus (may peace be upon them). Because many naïve Americans really don't study religion, they sometimes forget to check the facts. Many of them have no idea of the origin of the word "God" and where it originated. For example, "God is an old English word."

But for now, I cannot tell the truth. I will lose my job. I don't want to take this to my grave so I must continue lying to the American people. Just like before, we used the media to put fear in people's hearts. We were able to gain their trust and those who tried to get Americans to not believe the media didn't have a ground to stand own without funding. Now we are training Jews to go into ministry to teach Christians about their own faith. Every religion knows that we are the Chosen children though many stray off the path.

Let's look closely at how easy it is to say anything to people who truly trust their leaders. For example, Rev. John Hagee did a sermon that was a lie against God. Let's look at what he said in his sermon:

*Genesis 12:3: "And I will bless them that bless thee and curse him that curseth thee: and in thee shall all nations of the earth be blessed." Point: God has promised to bless the man or nation that blesses the Chosen People. History has proven beyond reasonable doubt that the Nations that have blessed the Jewish people have had the blessing of God; the Nations that have cursed the Jewish people have experienced the curse of God.*

People believed this lie without investigating John Hagee's claim. The truth was that in this verse Allah was speaking to Prophet Abraham: *"And I will bless them that bless thee, and curse him that curseth thee; and in thee shall all families of the earth be blessed"* (Genesis 12:3).

John Hagee stated, *"All Muslims have the mandate to kill Christian and Jews and it says so clearly in the Qur'an,"* which is also a lie; it doesn't say that in the Qu'ran—he only took part of the saying and not the entire saying. But if this was the case, then why haven't Muslims who converted to Islam killed their Christian and Jewish relatives? Why are Muslim men given permission to marry Christian and Jewish women? These non-Muslim women are not forced to convert to Islam. Many women who married Muslim men are still of the religion of their parents. It's just not permissible for a Muslim woman to marry a non-Muslim man because the man is the head of his household and a woman should follow the leadership of her husband.

The truth is that Muslims ask Allah to bless Prophet Ibrahim (Abraham) Peace Be Upon Him 5 five times a day. If we are truthful, then their claim would be valid, but we don't want to expose that Christians, Jews, and Muslims—all follow the laws of Abraham though the Christians and Jews may have altered the laws to benefit their own vain desires. I know Allah will deal with us justly. So if I should speak about Sharia law, then I need to speak about the laws in which we believe is from Allah, but we altered, changed, and updated our books to suit our own needs, where the Muslims will not change the laws in their Qu'ran. So, I must continue to misguide a people who hate, a people who are confused; a people who are naïve. Lies sells, and we will go broke in America if we are truthful.

FACTS

If we would follow the laws in our Books, they tell us:

Exodus 20:14: *"You shall not commit adultery.""*

Deuteronomy 22:22: *""If a man is found sleeping with another man's wife, both the man who slept with her and the woman must die.""*

Leviticus 20:10: *"If a man commits adultery with another man's wife—with the wife of his neighbor—both the adulterer and the adulteress must be put to death.""*

Proverbs 6:32: *"But a man who commits adultery lacks judgment; whoever does so destroys himself.""*

Jesus orders Christians to follow the Old Testament's laws: *"Do not think that I [Jesus] have come to abolish the Law (the Old Testament) or the Prophets; I have not come to abolish them but to fulfill them. I tell you the truth, until heaven and earth disappear, not the smallest letter, not the least stroke or a pen, will by any means disappear from the Law (the Old Testament) until everything is accomplished." (Mat. 5:17–18)*

*"Then Jesus said to the crowds and to his disciples: 'The teachers of the law and the Pharisees sit in Moses' seat. So you must obey them and do everything they tell you. But do not do what they do, for they do not practice what they preach.'" (Mat. 23:1–3)*

In the old days, punishment for adultery in Judaism was death, but now we have abandoned that law of Allah.

We have abandoned many of the laws of Allah. Usury/ interest is another practice that we are forbidden to deal with.

*Leviticus 25:36: "Do not take interest or any profit from them, but fear your God, so that they may continue to live among you."*

The same goes for Muslims' accordance with the Qu'ran and Sharia law.

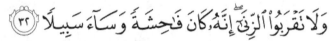

*"And do not approach unlawful sexual intercourse. Indeed, it is ever an immorality and is evil as a way." Qur'an 17:32*

According to Rense.com (http://www.rense.com/general44/ sevenjewishamericans.htm):

*"Today, seven Jewish Americans run the vast majority of US television networks, the printed press, the Hollywood movie industry, the book publishing industry, and the recording industry."*

# What Should Americans Look For In A President?

Our country was built on Christian "values and morals," but what happened? Like myself, anyone can have an opinion, and that's all it is—their own personal opinion. Some opinions can be backed up with facts. If I look at facts, I will say this country was built on Christian values and morals with a twist, and that twist depends on the benefactors. Who then are the benefactors? In my opinion, the benefactors are the majority, the ones who control America. Everything points to White Americans since the time the "Founding Fathers" developed the Constitution. It was very clear that the "Founding Fathers" were looking out for their people. Were some of the Founding Fathers religious men? Yes, of course they were. But each of them was brought up differently, and some were brought up on different faiths, though the majority of their faiths were under a Christian sect. What did they have in mind when they were in office and when they signed the Constitution? Was their decision based on the people's wishes or was it based on the people's votes?

*"Roger Sherman said: The question is, not what rights naturally belong to man, but how they may be most equally and effectually guarded in society. When you are in a minority, talk; when you are in a majority, vote."* (www. contitutionfacts.com).

Did you think the "Founding Fathers" would have ever thought a man of "color" would be the first president in history? In their Constitution, "Negroes" weren't Americans, nor could they vote. Truth be told, in my humble opinion, neither were Europeans Americans. However, was the war won or was it stolen? Either way, the claim that Christopher Columbus found America stayed in the history books. So when I think about America, it was a stolen country in which I was born to parents from many ethnicities, White, Indian, and Black Americans. I am just totally confused, but I can claim all sides. I laugh at myself at times and say, "What color do I want to claim today?" Let the truth be told: we all can claim a little this or a little that. Just look at the many slave children who were separated from their parents and the many girls and women who were raped by their "slave masters." Identity crisis exists in America; no one can really claim anything under the "Founding Fathers" who didn't set us free. It was during the Civil War that our real "Founding Father" Lincoln set the slaves free . . . fact or opinion?

Let's take a look at President Obama. He is hated by these "right-wing radical Christians." Imagine how they felt about President Lincoln for freeing the slaves. But keep in mind, this signed document on September 22, 1862, wouldn't have happened if the Union didn't win the war. What a bitter sweet day it was for millions of slaves, some who wanted freedom and others who were afraid to be freed. It was reported over 600,000 lives were lost. America has an outstanding history, a history that repeats itself. Therefore when we look at our government, we must ask ourselves the question, "Who is going to run our country like a country?"

I am a voter. I don't believe in all of my country's ways, but I love my country. Why do I vote when I am a devout Muslim . . . especially when a presidential candidate says, "I wouldn't vote for a Muslim president" and another candidate says, "Don't let Muslims in this country"? Be honest—that's their opinion. But what candidate Ben Carson must remember is that not too long ago, there were men in his family who couldn't vote at all because they were Black. It had nothing to do with their faith.

When I voted for President Obama, it wasn't because he was a man of "color"; it was because he stood on values and morals. But when he ran for office the second time, I felt he stood on principles that belonged to "another" people to get into office and that the values and morals that the religious community stood for were thrown out the window, and the religious community was ridiculed for adhering to the values and morals the "Founding Fathers" stood for. Our government truly destroyed our country's "principles, morals, and values"; they were "thrown under the bus". Everything was wrong with this country before President Obama was elected. In my humble opinion, President Bush sold the American people out long before President Obama took office. One president's mess became another president's nightmare!

I cannot lay all the blame on President Bush. He talked a good game too when he first ran for president. I almost went Republican, and with Ben Carson, I thought about it again. Donald Trump has a lot of guts and nerve, but I like him because he speaks his mind; it's clear what he is about. He is arrogant and unwise, but his character is out front, not hidden, no hidden agenda. He puts everything on the table of what he thinks about everyone; whether you like it or you don't, he doesn't give a damn! When I look at all the other presidential candidates, I am not convinced by any of them. I've learned from America's presidents, when I realized the importance of voting, that all of them can speak very well, they are convincing, and it appears they all have the people's best interests. But will they stand on the side of Allah? Will they truly stand on the side of Allah? Will they make this country a great Christian country like it should be or will they sell out to the devil? I know not everyone is Christian, and no, nor are we all from this country. However, if you study or visit other countries, you will find that the majority of the world is built on religious morals and values.

Why are Christians slowly being moved out of their own country for practicing their religion? America is the home of the free, giving people certain constitutional rights. People have the right to freedom of speech, religion, press, assembly, and petition. These are the rights of every citizen in the United States. So why did the Christians let this government remove Allah out of their laws? Why didn't Christians stand up for the laws of Allah? Why did they allow people to replace them with laws against Him? This isn't about same-sex marriage; this is about everything that is sinful. A country that was built on Christian morals and values will go out being known as a country that is built on what man determines to be correct morals and values based on who buys the presidential election, in my opinion, or who the president buys. These days, politicians are encouraging all the sins that make this country trillions of dollars each year. This is why it's so important to put emphasis on getting people to hate Islam and its people. If its certain "right wings", who truly hate all religion, then their mission is to take religion out of the constitution. If they can get non-thinkers to focus on getting a religion that the majority don't know anything about out of its country (America) then they can start a silent war to have religion removed, the same silent war that fought to have evil added to the law.

**Benjamin Franklin:** *"Our Constitution is in actual operation. Everything appears to promise that it will last. But in this world nothing is certain but death and taxes"* (www.contitutionfacts.com).

So what kind of president am I looking for? A president who is going to truly expose the truth, and a president who is going to speak on the truth and be just. I don't need a president who is going to say what I want to hear; I need a president who is going to fight for the rights of all people regardless of their race, sex, or religion, a president who is not going to be afraid to stand up for the laws of Allah and deny the laws against Him. I don't care what man you profess to be or what religion you claim; what I do care about is whether you will follow your Book. That's what is important. And if your Book speaks the truth, then live the truth. Don't fight against a religion that you clearly don't understand, and right now, I am talking about Islam. If you speak about Islam, then speak the truth; don't butter up the truth with falsehood for votes or to get people to turn against people of faith. The truth of the matter is if these lobbyists who are against the book of faith can get people to turn against others who truly are practicing Islam, Christianity, and Judaism, which are the main religions that seem to be always in conflict—truly you don't hear too much about other religions because they don't fall in the majority—if these lobbyists can get Christianity out of the picture, then they will be able to shut down all religions. At this point, the American people are too blind to see what is truly happening. One thing that Trump said was "Let them fight their own war." Well, in the 1700s, America had its own civil war; people weren't coming to America to fight the "rebels." Trump also said, "We need to bring back our jobs in America." Well, if the current and past Presidents took jobs out of prison and gave them to unemployed American citizens rather than allowing people to exploit those in the prison system, then America's economy will be in the green. But greed is America's biggest downfall. This is why sin is a trillion-dollar industry. Whoever runs for president needs to go to war against sin . . . In the end, you just might *WIN*.

It's so unfortunate that the laws of Allah are being ignored across the World. Every prophet was sent to his people to warn them, as well as to bring glad tidings of the promise of Allah. Nowadays, religious people have allowed themselves to be led astray blindly with, "It's okay because it's people of old who understood the Book before. Now it's a new day and we have to live a new life and change Allah words." *What*? How the heck do you allow people to misguide you?

Allah sent you the truth; why do wicked people have you believing lies, causing you to turn against people, causing you to be racist toward a group of people who are trying to live a righteous life?

Even with Kim Davis—she stood her ground as one who believes in the laws of Allah. She refused to abide by man's law that was recently put in effect and is clearly against the laws of Allah; she stood firm that she could not go against her religious faith. Because of her strong belief in the laws of Allah, she was arrested.

What would you do? I applaud her for standing for what she believes in. May Allah bless her to remain strong and continue to stand firm.

Wake up, religious people! There is a large following behind Trump, because they are the ones who dislike a people they don't understand. But look at the bigger picture: if they come for us, they soon will come for you and when all is said and done, religion will be removed in the Constitution and evil will take over again. Even when other religious people come from you, make sure they are "real religious" people. Because real Muslims aren't the ones who commit hideous crimes; they are the ones who fight a fair war. They don't kill innocent men and women, the same with Christians . . . but if both parties should fight, then it must be *JUST*!

# Why Do I Believe Islam Is The Hope For America?

Did I tell you that I was born into a Christian (Methodist) family? I believed, like so many, that I had the best family. I loved my grandmother; she was such a good Christian woman. My Christian religion led me to Islam.

Unfortunately, Americans put people into office in Washington who make bad decisions about their lives. Morals begin to slowly fade, and the things that mean something, such as family values and morals, begin to fade too. Prostitution, gambling, drugs, alcoholism, adultery, and homosexuality begin to grow in numbers all under the disguise of Christianity. In Republican states, the White society hates Blacks so much that they make it very hard on Black men, women, and their children every step of the way. Everything that was made to assist Blacks to get ahead in life was stripped away by bills in favor of white families. Black farmers have a hard time, and more of a difficult time, paying taxes on their lands. Many of the farmers' children are encouraged by their parents to become doctors, lawyers, and teachers from the time they are in elementary school. Parents instilled these ideas in their heads while White teachers discouraged little Black children from even thinking about being anything other than farmers or servants. The only thing most blacks were good for in the eyes of Whites was entertainment only, and this is what brought them joy: to listen to us sing, dance, and play instruments until we started playing in their sports professionally. They discouraged Black children from almost everything, even life skills. They taught their children life skills such as hunting, fishing, swimming, and archery.

Life around us is changing. We didn't have all the distractions that we have now. Children were so innocent. Nowadays, innocence is thrown out the window. When America cared about saving their children from the ill of society, they made sure their girls was married off, between the ages of 7 and 12 in the early years (1600s) in America, with the consent of parents, but consummation took place when the girl reached puberty. Look at the hypocrisy in our own backyard. Isn't it something else? Even the way we dress in America—the women were covered and wore skirts and/or dresses down to their ankles. In our Christian country, fornication was forbidden, along with every law that Allah made. So, what happened to our country?

I do agree with changing some laws because they are laws against Allah. Nowadays, it's man's laws against Allah's. Many Americans want to use the laws of Allah to suit their own purposes.

This brings me to why I feel that Islam is a solution for America. Let me be clear: I believe that the religion itself can help American people work toward righteousness within their own faiths. You hear people saying they don't want "Sharia Law," but do they really understand Sharia Law? For the sake of argument, there may be certain laws within the Book which we can agree to disagree on. The truth of the matter is that in most cases, people don't want to give up their sinful ways.

If a law is about pleasing Allah and staying away from sin, why wouldn't you want to adhere to that law? In reality, many of our laws came from the Holy Book here in America. For example, the citizens of an Islamic country adheres to the law of their book, they are ridiculed for following their book. When it is clearly the same in the Books of the Christians and Jews?

Many people say Jesus (pbuh) died for their sins. But what's mind-boggling is, did Jesus tell people to keep sinning? So out of nowhere, a Jewish minister said to his congregation, which I will assume was American, "We must *NOT* continue to let the Muslims in our country." But this is a country where his parents weren't born in, and what's even more mind-boggling is that the Jewish minister's parents didn't believe that Jesus (pbuh) came to their people as of yet, but they (Jews) do believe Jesus (pbuh) will be coming back to earth but not to the Christians regardless of what has been told in the Injeel (Gospel). Also, the Muslims believe Jesus (pbuh) will return. Please read Quran, surah 3 verse 55.

Many people loved Muslims in the early years in America; even in a dance book, *"Swing"*, which was published in the early '60s, they had a dance that was called "Allahu Akbah" Another mind-boggling thing, and even more interesting, is that America's liars have deceived the people again; they lied to make America's people believe that Islam is one of the worst religions and that we must get it out of America.

But the truth of the matter is, just like before with China, Korea, Spain, and Africa, deals and treaties were set up, and only America's government can have a monopoly on "weapons of mass destruction," only America can drop atomic bombs on an entire country, only America can bully other countries and bomb them, just like so many times, taking life after life, but on the other hand, America's government spends so much money on buying skills, talents, goods, and services from other countries. America's government will cheat its own people of opportunities and development. *Why?* Because they *CONTROL* the minds of so many Americans so they cannot see or think. There are so many people in other countries that hate us Americans, and they are *NOT* Muslim, though the focus is Muslims or

Islam at this time. But truth be told, there are so many people who hate us (our government). When I was in England, it bothered me when I saw a protest sign held up speaking out against America. I snapped a picture of this protest. They weren't Muslims. Korea's government wants to go to war against America so bad that it continues to tell America's government they have "weapons of mass destruction" and they're not afraid to take us or any other country on (in war).

But now we have so many people from all walks of life moving to America. But what is interesting is that once America destroys a country, they rebuild that country and change that country's laws (democracy) to suit the needs of many Americans who will be moving there. Someone knows the truth; America has a stronghold in these countries and has them under the banner of "fighting terrorism." Do you know how many innocent people our own government has wiped out in these countries? I smell a *VERY LARGE RAT*! American people, we must stop and think. Before it was "war against terrorism" starting with 9/11. Many Americans traveled and lived in Islamic countries, and they saw the beauty of other faiths, family morals, and values— things that America lost.

There are a group of Americans who are out to do something about the many White Americans who either live or lived in those beautiful religious countries, where people of faith are able to live, share, and do good work together. These Americans see a life in another country that offers traditional morals and values. But these evildoers don't want that information shared. These evildoers don't want to keep intact values and morals nor a religion that focuses on family life and the marriage between a man and woman for the reproduction of life itself. They don't want a religion that tells us the punishment for crimes, a religion that teaches us how to treat our women, a religion that explains what a disbeliever truly is and how to treat our neighbors and our families. These *were* once laws in the Christian faith, which I left; this was the faith I once saw in my Christian household. But again, Americans, Americans, know exactly what to do to deceive a beautiful country and rob the American people. Now we Americans must pay for the rebuilding of a country that our government contributed to destroying, under the banner of "fighting terrorism" (Bush administration). Our country basically wiped out an entire country (please insert country's name) under that banner and then fought to stop "weapons of mass destruction" which, by the way, both our country and Korea have, yet our country avenged the killing of American Christians and Muslims who worked and/or died trying to save lives. Three thousand innocent lives to killing two hundred thousand and we wonder why? You fill in the blanks.

Americans spend billions on waste, foolishness, illegal drugs and sex, but refuse to spend billions to help the America economy.

But before the war against "terrorism," so many Americans lived, worked, and worshipped in those Islamic countries. America's government convinced Islamic countries to give the American people what they're used to, "keep them intoxicated with swine, alcohol, cigarettes, illegal sex, and entertainment," but unfortunately, many Islamic governments sold out their religion to the deceivers, just like the people of old in many countries. Mind you, before the war was won between the believers and disbelievers, the true followers of Prophet Moses? (pbuh) cleaned up people's minds from idol worship, intoxication, illegal sex, homosexuality, gambling, eating unlawful food, killing sons and letting girls live, enslaving girls, and most of all, the worship of gods other than Allah. Our Prophets, peace be unto them all, were sent to their respective people, and our beloved Prophet Muhammad (pbuh) was sent to all mankind to enhance what the Prophets have done before him: cleaning up the filth in those countries, signing treaties, teaching people, and fighting clean wars where not one innocent civilian was murdered. The mistake that some of the Islamic governments made was allowing America's government to convince them to allow this poison (what Allah has forbidden) to take over their Islamic countries. The Islamic governments became easy prey for America to take over under the banner of "fighting terrorism."

Many religious people bought into immoral behavior. Their minds were intoxicated from the poison. They no longer could see what just happened. Americans have been able to convince other Americans through media that Islam is bad, saying it in a way to cloud the minds of many non-thinkers. Then, American media would soon tell the people, "It's not all Muslims, it's some Muslims." But the damage has been done. Instead of saying "some men did such and such," they said, "some Muslim terrorists did such and such," the same way they treated "Black Americans" once they were freed and had rights similar to the Europeans. The media portrayed Blacks as evil, cursed, bad people who terrorize White families.

They utilize the words "Islam" and "Muslims" hoping to make Muslims feel ashamed of being Muslims, and then they treat Muslim women and their children the same way they did to so many Black Americans.

What is the truth? Why do we want America's people to tell the truth? Well, I am American, born and raised, my father's genes were a mixture of white blood and Indian blood, and my mother's had a mixture of black and Indian. What I do know is we cannot continue this way in America. It will be a matter of time before we will become the victims. We are sitting ducks, and unfortunately, ignorance is a disease.

We must stop letting people feed us anything and we must start investigating the truth and ask questions and vote to put the right people in office who are not easily bought or willing to sell us. WE must take back America, not by mistreating innocent people, but by securing the lives of righteous people and locking up people who are the real criminals, not because of the color of their skin or because they have a different faith, but because they broke the laws.

Islam is a religion for all people. Just know I am not trying to get you to become a Muslim; I am trying to get you to pray to whom Jesus prayed to, to walk like Christ, and to stop sinning. Just like America's government created radical Christians, Americans have helped to create these radical Muslims and radical Jews, Chinese, Mexicans, Hispanics, Indians, and so on and so forth, and if we look closer, we will see that Americans played a part in it, directly or indirectly.

Together we can save America, but we first must understand that sin is a trillion-dollar industry that is destroying America and its people. Stop letting any religious leader tell you anything without proof, and when they use the Qur'an to be witness to their lies, know they are cursing themselves and those who follow them. The words have never been altered or changed, but those in the Bible have been altered so many times by man to fit their own vain desires. Read the truth, and then follow the truth. Live by the laws of your own Book as revealed by Our Lord!

This is my own theory and my own opinion. No one influenced me or paid me to write this information.

I know there are some of you who have a sick mind and hate it when people use their freedom of speech. That's all it is. If you're not that person and don't have that type of character, leave it alone. For those of you who have a problem with this book, I pray that Allah open your hearts and remove the veil from your eyes. It's not that serious; for real, it's not! Everyone will have their own opinion, views, and beliefs, and that is okay—we all do. We are human beings. The truth is that the whole world belongs to Allah; this is His creation, and if you don't believe in a Higher Power, that's okay. That is you, not me. We are taught "you go your way and I go mine." I am not here to convince you. I am not even trying to convert you. I only can ask Allah to do His will. But know this, we all will return to the earth regardless of how long scientists and doctors believe they can keep people alive; we all will die. If you are truthful, then keep yourself from dying or from illness without utilizing things in which spiritual people or religious people say is from Allah. Don't use grains of rice, water, animals, and other nutritional substances that will keep you alive; don't even utilize the air that you breathe daily. If you are truthful, don't utilize anything that is on earth. Lock yourself up in a sealed house with no lights, water, gas, or food, and board up all the windows and vents where not one ounce of air can leak through. Let's see how long you can survive without utilizing what is from the "God" that you don't believe in.

No man can buy life. A man's money may keep him from suffering. However, when God is ready for you, you will return to Him, and not an ounce of medication or a dollar will keep you from Him. If you don't die when the doctor calls it, it just wasn't your time.

# Developing A Strong Foundation For Yourself And Family

Develop a strong foundation for yourself and for your family; if your family members stray off the path, feel blessed because you have set a strong foundation for your family to return to.

Everyone comes from two in this life—a man and a woman—regardless of what one may think. I am not here to debate what one should think and/or should or shouldn't be or do. I am only here to write what is on my mind and to challenge us to do what is right.

This book may not be for you; I wrote it for people who are serious about changing their lives. I am writing for religious people who are in business or want to start up a business, while at the same time holding on to their principles, morals, and values. I want to encourage you to believe in yourself and keep the faith in your Lord. This world is only temporary, and none of these material things will go with you when you return to your Lord. Ask yourself this question: "Do I want to carry the sins of others with me to my grave, do I want to contribute to their bad habits such as alcohol, drugs, gambling, and illegal sex?"

If you said no, then proceed to the next chapter of this book. We will work together to develop your ideas that will be lawful in the eyes of Allah.

# It's All About Business

Why did I put this chapter together? Because it is all about business, and I know I don't want to leave this world without trying to make my country great. I believe in the power of Allah, and I believe everything is possible. I may not be able to save the world, but I can at least try to reach those people who are like me, and those people who want to save our next generation by introducing lawful products and services.

I love being creative and coming up with ideas. If I could go back in time, I would have loved to share the things that I'd learned from my mother and my grandmother. They were my best friends; both were very supportive and encouraging.

I have no regrets, and if I did, there is nothing I can do about it. I only can live in the present and work toward the future and take the good I learned from my past and apply it now.

I am grateful that I have overcome several obstacles that were blocking me from moving forward in my writing. I released my first book in 2009; six years later, I released my second book, which you're reading. I am striving to become a billionaire, and I am hoping that Allah blesses me to become one. This is what I want for myself, and I hope it's in Allah's Plan for this to happen and to not let it be a test for me.

I believe a person can be whatever they want to be if they strive for it. I do believe if I strive for it, Allah will do the rest.

When I first went into business, a receptionist at Atlanta's business license office told me that I couldn't start up a business without having a college degree in business. I didn't listen and I started up my first business. What she did not know is that she challenged me, and I was determined to show her that I could start up a business without a degree. Nowadays, however, I would encourage people to obtain some type of certificate or degree in any field of business of their interest; it wouldn't hurt. It will only enhance their knowledge.

Never let anyone steal your joy. If you want to do something lawful, go for it. If it's for you, Allah will not let it pass you by. If it's not, then it will pass you by.

My advice to anyone who wants to go into business is to learn as much as you can before starting one, especially if you do not plan on going to college to obtain a business degree.

There are a lot of business books out there. Nowadays you can always depend on Google to help you look up, research, and/or find a business for sale. In other words, there is no reason a person cannot learn as much as they can about starting a business before embarking on it. If you're serious, then study, make those little sacrifices, and you may even take up an online course.

And please surround yourself with positive people who have the same dreams as you, who want to be pleasing to Allah and earn an honest and lawful living.

# Working Toward Success

It's everyone's goal to become successful in the things that they do. It all starts during childhood, when you had to learn how to make a parent come to you to pick you up, to change your clothes when you're wet, to feed you when you're hungry or in pain. You would cry! You had to learn to crawl; you tried very hard not to fall. A child takes its first steps, trembling as he or she tries to lift his or her left foot off the floor. He or she says their first word: "ma-ma" or "da-da." One thing we learn is that children must take steps toward perfecting how to crawl, walk, and talk.

This is the way I feel about business. A business will go through stages as it is being built. Our goal is to help you work toward success, and in doing so, we must first learn to work together. By working together, we will be helping one another succeed.

Learning to want the best for others is important. Everyone wants to succeed, and everyone must work toward succeeding. Most people's mistake is concentrating on what others are doing for success. No one runs a business the same; maybe the concept is the same, but it is run differently. And don't concentrate on other people's money. Remember, their money is their money no matter how they made it.

Some people have worked and sweated for a company, and by doing so, they find themselves angry about building someone else's dream or business while only earning minimum wages. But I want you to always remember, you agreed to work for those wages, and by doing so, you gave a service and were paid for that service.

Learning to get more for your work is important, however, as with anything you are giving a service and getting paid for your service.

Let's touch on the real issue: "I want to get paid!"

What does this mean? Most people who are in business want to get paid. When people only want to get "paid," their business eventually dies. Why, because they want to get paid, and guess what? They will get paid. These are the people who find themselves living from paycheck to paycheck or spending on one major sale and waiting for the next one.

"I want to be successful." What is your meaning of success? Let's look at the definition of success: the achievement of something, a favorable outcome, accomplishment, achievement, profit, progress, prosperity.

There are several things I want you to know about working toward success. This is not a quick way to get rich, though you may find some people who have gotten rich really fast. However, without the right guidance, they will go broke just as fast.

You may open up a business because you're saying you are tired of working for someone else. Just remember you will be going to work for yourself, and working for yourself is "WORK", be it selling products or providing a service. Repeat after me: "If it is the will of Allah, *I WILL BE SUCCESSFUL*"

# It's All About Business (Getting Started)

## Introduction

There are over 28 million businesses today. The majority of these businesses started out from an idea. The key to an *idea* is making it a reality! There are many people in today's society tired of working for other people and feel they are being overworked and underpaid! The purpose of this book is to help people who are tired of working for a company that does not have any real value to them, except for receiving a meager paycheck. This book serves three purposes:

1. *HELPING YOU DEVELOP YOUR IDEA,*
2. *MAKING IT WORK*
3. *GETTING PAID FOR YOUR SERVICES*

What I want you to do before you start reading this chapter is to think about why you purchased this book. I will advise you not to read this chapter unless you're truly ready to *GET STARTED!* Remember, *IT'S NOT PERSONAL*; rather, *IT'S ALL ABOUT BUSINESS!*

To hire employees to get the job done at a fast pace, companies must pay out very little without going broke while helping people earn a living. Families are being torn apart because of lack of money, and teens are forced to work because of lack of money in their household. In many of these cases, children are cheated out of their education. That brings us right back to where we started: getting paid for our services. Taking on a second job is a must sometimes, enabling you to make enough money to pay your bills.

Still there are things left undone. It is impossible to focus on your family when you have to make a living. *IDEA!* I keep repeating *IDEA* because there are so many people with great ideas; however, they don't know how to put those ideas into action. Take a moment out and read this book. Together, we can open your mind and explore your ideas. *Remember one thing; nothing comes easy!*

# Chapter One

## Ideas

For centuries and for years to come, people will continue to have ideas, and some of these ideas will turn into money-making ventures. You will have a choice at this point! Will your idea be rewarding to you, your family, and your community? You will discover that when things are rewarding to you, they will be rewarding for your family and help you meet the needs of your community.

With this in mind, you will gain the understanding you need to learn about your ideas and the realization of your ideas, their purpose, and their benefits. Ideas are things that a person has thought about that will serve a need. For example, before there were vehicles, people rode camels and horses. Then one day, someone thought of how to get from place to place faster than by riding animals.

A bright idea surfaced in one's mind: "if man could fly like a bird." This person began to study how birds flew, and from that idea, he realized that if a person could fly like a bird, it could satisfy a need, so he came up with an aircraft with wings. This invention began from an idea. From that one idea came engines, motors, and cars, and because of that idea, a family as well as the community profited. *It all started from an idea.* This idea created jobs in communities and incomes for families. Ask yourself this question: will your idea be of benefit to you, your family, and your community?

This is how you can measure your idea. Once you come up with your idea, write it down on paper and study it, then begin conducting your own research. This may take days, months, or even a year, but you will discover one or more things about your idea. Is it unique and beneficial to you, your family, and your community? Notice that I continue to add "your community." Why? Remember, the purpose of coming up with an idea is to benefit from it, and to do so, it must be sellable. Those who will buy or support your ideas are your consumers, and the consumers are your customers, and your customers come from communities, and your customers can also be your clients. On another note: businesses make up communities.

Nowadays everyone wants to make money, and everyone wants to be successful in life. When I think of business, I think of ideas that will be good products to market or good services to render. How will I benefit, how will my family benefit, and how will my community benefit from my idea? Now remember one important aspect: all ideas may be good no matter what you come up with; you must record it on paper, conduct research, and make sure that it is marketable.

Your ideas are your own thoughts. Don't try to find people to approve or implement your ideas. You must start your own ideas independently. Every individual has his or her own dreams, so look for support only when you've implemented your idea.

Don't get distracted by negative forces. Block them out. You must start by being around people who want to succeed and are inspired to have something better out of life. Remember, always keep Allah first, trust in Him, and work as if it all depends on you . . . Allah will do the rest.

Allah will let us experience as much as we can handle! I will share with you some of my personal experience in starting my business, as well as my successes and my setbacks once I implemented my ideas. I never thought about just myself; I also thought about my family and friends before I put an idea in motion. I always offered my family and friends encouragement "to think and grow a rich attitude." I felt we all would be able to gain from my ideas and visions. To do so, they must be willing to take a risk, have spare time, have a vision, and most of all, have faith, not in me, but in the Creator.

My idea started off while I was playing with my newborn baby. I was thinking what would be nice for him. This was my firstborn. My thoughts went from garments to toys, but the time I had my third child was when I decided to start pursuing my ideas. I wanted to have a money-making idea, an idea that will allow me to work from home. Many ideas were implemented from people's homes; believe me, home-based businesses have been around for a very long time. What I thought about was having a small *in-home day care*. I looked into having a home day care for toddlers. Personally, I had a fear of dealing with newborns; their needs were a lot greater than those of toddlers. Furthermore, with two toddlers and one infant, I didn't want to be neglectful.

Once I started looking into obtaining my license, I learned there weren't as many restrictions as I previously thought. This was in the early 1980s. It wasn't until the late '80s when the restrictions came about because of unsafe nurseries and negligence. Because of this, it became harder for people who wanted to go into day care businesses to obtain licenses.

For those who are looking to open up a nursery, if this is something that you would like to pursue, don't allow the restrictions to stop you. Go ahead and do whatever it takes to get started. Your nursery may become unique. Think about what you can offer that no other day cares are offering. I came up with the idea of running a twenty-four-hour weekend day care accommodating parents or friends who needed a good caregiver while they were out of town or just needed a break without disturbing friends or relatives or being disappointed.

I did this only on Fridays and Saturdays. During weekdays, I operated a regular day care for toddlers. I offered hands-on activities, such as finger painting and learning the alphabet and numbers. During the time I had my in-home day care for toddlers, Georgia Pre-K programs weren't in existence. I am a witness that children as young as three years of age can learn basic arithmetic. My busiest moments were on the weekends. The twenty-four-hour service paid off; it brought in just as much money as it did during the weekdays.

I enjoyed every bit of it until it interfered with my family time. The father of my children was happy about me starting a business from home, and he said he really didn't have a problem with it and he was very supportive in the beginning. He didn't want me to work outside of the home. At the same time, he knew I wanted to have my own money. This was the first time I operated my own home-based business. I realized operating a business in your home can interfere with your family life.

It can be difficult to separate family from business when your business is being run in your home. Although it starts off with good intentions, somehow it becomes a problem. No matter how good the money may seem, home should be a place you can come to for peace of mind after work or after dealing with others. My children's father felt as if others whom he wasn't responsible for was taking up his space. I started feeling uncomfortable because of him feeling the way that he did. I gave my parents two weeks' notice so they could make other childcare arrangements.

For those of you who have an interest in operating a home day care business, please research the requirements as changes are being made every year. When starting a home day care service, make sure you have a split-level home or a large basement so you can separate your family from your home-based business. Also, consider having a separate entrance to your home. If it's a home day care, make sure you have a secure private fenced backyard and secure playground equipment. Once you've acquired your childcare license, completed the childcare and CPR course, and secured your home, then you want to set up activities. It's imperative for you to set up rules and regulations; keep in mind that these children are a trust, and they are loved by their parents. Make sure the children are being signed in with a body checklist; you and the parents check if there are visible fresh marks on the child's arms, face, back, head, legs, and feet. You need to mark it on paper in front of the parents and let them sign the sheet acknowledging there are or there are no visible marks on their child's body. Do this at sign in and sign out. Protect yourself always, because nowadays there are many ills in our society among families. Set up your activities through the week, purchase a calendar, and stick by your calendar.

Second, offer breakfast, lunch, and snacks. If you plan on having a weekend day care in addition to your regular day care, make sure you have a day or two set aside for you and your family.

Third, Friday would be a good day to have an overnight service, especially during the holiday season. I would offer extended hours during the holiday season and take time to do special artwork with children, teaching them to make gifts or greeting cards for their parents. Children enjoy doing things for their parents or putting on a special play or dinner for their parents during the season. Lastly, give parents a contract that includes rules and regulations to follow. Protect yourself as well. I pray you will have a successful business.

My second idea and venture was a children's clothing store with my friend. I still operated out of my home. I had a good-sized house, although it was only a one-level home. The rooms were extremely big with high ceilings. We contracted out seamstresses to sew for us and also went to kids' outlet warehouses and hosiery outlets to purchase undergarments and socks. We obtained our business license and opened the shop using the money I've saved and my friend's income tax refund. We were able to open an account with United Notches and Kids Unlimited. As I stated in the beginning, Allah makes no mistakes; everything we do in life Allah allows us to experience, and hopefully what we've learned we're able to share with others.

We operated what we believed to be a successful business for one year, and we learned something very important, that you should not trust everyone with your business. My friend and I were so happy about our new venture together. I remember it like it was yesterday; we were sitting on her auntie's steps talking about investing in a business. While we were brainstorming, I thought about something for children. This is when we said "a children clothing store"; immediately, we went into action. We agreed on a name: "Ummies (Mothers) Place." When we came together to embark on this business, we had several things in common: we both had children, and we were both concerned that we couldn't find clothes that were appropriate for our children. Though I had daughters and she had sons, we had friends who complained about not finding modest children's clothing. The garments many Muslim parents look for are nice overgarments for girls and/or longer dresses and ankle-length skirts. For our boys, we wanted them to dress in garments that were in the Eastern style. We couldn't find these types of garments, so we hired sisters who were seamstresses to custom-make the boys' and girls' garments.

We were able to provide our customers the clothes, undergarments, and much more that they wanted for their children. We did very well the first year; the second year, our sales began to drop, not because people didn't like our products but we weren't able to keep up with these demands. Why, because we trusted people to produce the custom-made garments, which were our number one product.

Our last seamstress failed us terribly. It cost us our customers and caused us to lose money. Because of this, someone else immediately took the advantage to open up shop. We learned so many valuable lessons from this major mistake. Unless your contractor is working on-site, don't let your merchandise out of your eyesight. This was a big mistake; once we had let the fabric out of our possession, we had a very hard time getting the fabric back regardless of the numerous attempts to retrieve our merchandise from the seamstress' home. One day, we sat outside her door all day until she either left her house or returned; this was the only time we were able to retrieve our merchandise, and it took us two weeks to run into her. Once we did retrieve the fabric, it was too late: the bolts of fabric we had given her had all been cut out. It was very difficult to find another seamstress to sew the cutout fabric. We became very disappointed, and we became discouraged so we closed our doors to Ummies Place. We also learned that you must secure your own business; not everyone is going to value your business the way you do.

Always have a business contract, and only contract out a person who depends on this contract for their livelihood and business. Remember, if this is only a hobby, then you will get a "hobby worker," meaning they're not depending on this work for a source of income to fulfill their and their family's needs.

Remember one thing: just because someone wants you to take them seriously does not mean they are going to apply the same rules to themselves.

It is imperative that you follow through with your contract. Moreover, if the other party's end of that contract is not honored after that contract is signed, don't hesitate taking them to small-claims court to compensate for the breach of their contractual promise.

Remember, whenever you purchase anything with a company on credit, you are under a contract. We did not take our seamstress to small-claims court, and as a result, we lost fabric, time, and capital gain! Our business began to drop because we did not have garments, and we reluctantly asked our customers to come back the following week. I will advise anyone who wants to start a retail business, especially if it will require you to outsource the work, to make sure the person(s) is trustworthy be family or friends; it's so important to secure your business.

With regard to credit, it has its advantages and disadvantages. You may be helping your customers, but are your customers helping you? In other words, don't give away anything you can't afford to lose. This doesn't only apply to credit; it also does to money as well. Personally, I don't borrow money from people who I know can't afford to wait for me to pay them back. I make sure the person who is extending a loan to me understands I don't have a specific date or time to repay their money.

However, I do make intentions to repay him or her in the near future. If you borrow money from a bank, versus borrowing money from someone that you know who is able to extend or wait, you have thirty days before your first payment with interest is due, unless you pay the entire amount within thirty days without making monthly installments.

Retail falls under sales. You must be a virtuous seller who can trade any product. I learned how to sell the clothes off a person's back, so I'll go on to say I never gave up on having my own business. I always believed anything that Allah has for you won't miss you, and when it did not work out, I was still grateful to Allah for the experiences.

After closing the children's clothing store, I decided to pursue being a Tupperware distributor. It was a contract between Tupperware and me. I agreed to sell their products, and they agreed they would pay me a commission from my sales, and it would become an opportunity to advance professionally. Tupperware allowed me to be my own boss; I was blessed to learn how to build a good distributor team. I learned how to market and had the pleasure of networking with other entrepreneurs. I enjoyed working for Tupperware, and I had no complaints. I learned a valuable lesson while I was a distributor, and that was not to buy as much as I sold. Tupperware pushed their distributors to move up by giving them incentives such as driving a company car or van and the opportunity to travel.

Never buy products or encourage your team to buy products themselves just for you to be the top seller for the month or to hold on to your car. You will find yourself going broke, and in the end, you will lose out on the car.

This is what I learned from Tupperware, and I thank God for my experience in the sales industry. I also became a Tupperware manager and drove off in a new station wagon, and when I couldn't maintain the sales quota, I had to turn in the keys. Therefore, don't become attached to the incentives because you may not always be able to uphold your sales quota. Your sales are what pay for the car.

After Tupperware, I decided to become an Avon distributor, where I found myself doing the same thing. I purchased from my sales, and I could not make it, but I enjoyed working as an Avon representative and enjoyed their products. However, I wasn't able to achieve managerial status. Nevertheless, I had a good time meeting new people and using both Avon and Tupperware products; both businesses still allowed you to work at your own pace, giving you that sense of being "self-employed."

I have a friend who became one of the top Avon distributors. She has traveled with Avon to many places, and she also has enjoyed their products. Because of her creativity, she was able to climb her way to the top, by the will of Allah; she used to own a gift shop, and most of her gift baskets contained Avon products. It can work!

Well, as I said before, I thank Allah for all that He allowed me to experience. I am very grateful. After working in the sales industry, I returned to working with children since I have children of my own. However, at the time, my children were not old enough to participate in some of the activities. I enjoyed doing things for children. It wasn't about the money for the most part; in most cases, it was because children needed trustworthy caregivers who really cared, and I felt that I am one of those people.

This brings me to my next idea. I decided to open a summer camp for children aged 6–12. At the time, my children were aged 4, 3, 2 years old, and 3 months. I thought about them, but at the same time, I wanted children aged 6 and older. The summer camp I operated was a nonprofit camp. I wasn't looking to get rich; my objective was to provide a needed service in my community. It wasn't just for underserved children; the camp was to serve all children.

In my opinion, all children are at risk regardless of race, sex, and religion. When I reached out to my friend Anthonette to inform her that I wanted to open a summer camp, and have her as my partner, she thought it was a good idea. I contacted the City for the requirements to move forward with my project. After explaining my business plan to the woman who answered the phone, she immediately informed me that I didn't have the credentials to open a camp because I did not have a degree in Childhood Development.

My reply was "thank you," and I hung up the phone. I do understand one thing: everyone who has come up with an invention or a sellable idea didn't have a college degree, and if I let some lady who just sits behind a desk answering phones intimidate me from pursuing my ideas, then too bad for me. Nonetheless, I love challenges, so I continued to do my research and asked plenty of questions. And one day, my neighbor saw me, and I shared with him my planned endeavor. He instructed me to contact a minister who was part of the Atlanta youth program "Save the Children Task Force."

I tried reaching out to the minister several times but was unsuccessful. My neighbor then advised me to contact the department that had the program "Save the Children Task Force." He told me to ask for the person who was in charge of that program. I did and I succeeded, though I never made contact with the minister who was well liked. All I did was mention the minister's name, and they provided me with an abundance of information. I was also put in touch with the person in charge of that program, and immediately he asked me how the minister was doing.

I didn't lie by saying he was fine; I just said I hadn't spoken to him. He asked me what could he do for me, and I explained my mission to him. He then instructed me to forward him a copy of my proposal, and we started from there. I did exactly what he asked me to do. I put the information together for my friend so she could put it into a proposal. My friends couldn't believe it. My words to her, "Never say never." We were on first base now.

While she was writing the proposal, I was looking for a site to start this summer program. I found an alternative school, and the principal was delighted to accommodate us for that summer. I was very excited! I knew we needed start-up capital. I came up with the idea to have a winter carnival. We sold tickets for 50 cents. We sold tickets at malls and stores. We advertised everywhere; we hung signs on every telegraph pole we could possibly think of. One place where we put up a sign was on Pryor Street in front of a Church's Chicken that is now closed. I remember it vividly: we were hanging up signs, and the next thing we knew, we were in the middle of a shootout right in the parking lot of Church's Chicken. One of the guys involved was in front of our truck. Anthonette was driving, and we placed the babies on the floor of the truck. Both babies were six months old.

There were bullets flying over our heads. Anthonette cranked up the truck and started driving off, the shooter jumped out of the way! We didn't look back. We just continued driving, and right to this day, we have no idea what happened. When we returned home, we discovered there were several bullet holes in the cab of the truck. Thank Allah, we were shielded from those bullets. We never went back in that area; we no longer wanted their support. We sold booth spaces, and we monopolized the hot dog stand and soda. We had a successful winter carnival and grossed $4,500 just in that one day.

I submitted the proposal to "Save the Children Task Force." I remember it was last-minute; I had to walk-in. I was invited to come to the task force meeting where they would be awarding recipients. That day, I was so excited about attending. I had no idea what the outcome was going to be. But on that day, I was prepared to speak about the West End Summer Camp. I walked in confidently as I stood by the elevator. The man I was looking to talk to stood beside me, and he introduce himself to me. "Hi, I am Reverend M." I was so happy to see him. "It's so good finally meeting you. I've been trying to reach you. My neighbor told me to reach you, but I ended up speaking to Mr. S. about my summer program that I am trying to open in the West End," I said with the biggest smile, walking to the elevator. He asked, "Did you speak to Mr. S.?" "Yes," I replied, and when the elevator opened up, Mr. S. was standing at the door. He greeted us both. "I see you and Ms. Jihad are together?" We smiled and we walked into the meeting. I had my flyers and my game face. Not knowing what to expect, I saw a panel of 12 people: 10 whites and 2 blacks. They were making the announcements about the grant awardees. I believe this was in 1987, and they were giving out $30,000 to $100,000 for summer programs. After they finished awarding the recipients, they then introduced me. Mr. S. told the panel about my proposal and why he was for the proposal, then he asked for the panel to vote and to let him know if there were any questions and/or any reason why the proposal should be rejected. Well, the only Black woman there raised her hand, and the first thing she said was that she would like to reject the proposal, and the reason she gave was that the city of Atlanta has programs for underserved children and that the funding was being given to the Boys and Girls Club, and she didn't see a need to fund a summer camp in the city of Atlanta. She ended with, "Therefore, I oppose funding this summer program." Mr. S. asked me if I wanted to say something to the panel before they voted. I stood up, and I looked directly at the lady on the panel. I said, "Yes," as I was distributing the flyers. I turned to the panel and said, "She is absolutely right that the city has plenty of summer programs in Atlanta. However, every program that is held is in the heart of the projects including the Boys and Girls Club, leaving children who do not live in the housing projects nowhere to go therefore they become 'lock-keyed children' or easy prey. Drug dealers are not recruiting children who live in the projects, they are recruiting children who don't live in the projects. My point is that every child doesn't live in the projects, and I am fighting for those children." After I presented my case, the people in the audience gave me a standing ovation. The panel voted for our proposal, and we were awarded $30,000 for the first summer.

We opened up the summer camp starting off with the working capital that we raised. We had children from every household with their parents, who were doctors, lawyers, and police officers from middle- and underserved families. We charged everyone the same rate, $15 per week, and that included tutoring the children in language arts, math, and reading. We also took the children on field trips every Thursday. We had a "walk against drugs" rally, an arts festival where the children profited from selling their artwork. We operated the summer camp successfully for three years. After that, I fell ill. I had to have lung surgery; I was hospitalized for two months.

Allah truly blessed me to live and see many of my ideas flourish. I had first-hand experience in becoming an entrepreneur at an early age. My first business venture, I was 21. Because of that experience, I learned about non-profit organizations and how to write proposals. Additionally, I was able to help others who wanted to start their own non-profit organization. I wanted the summer camp to continue, and I was hoping that my friends would be able to carry on without me. It was difficult for me the following summer.

I learned another valuable lesson: my dream isn't everyone else's dream. I wanted so much for the summer camp to continue; my friends were able to manage as far as they could. Which brings me to say, make for certain that you find people, whether it's a friend or associate, who share the same interests. My friends were there to help me and support me, but it wasn't a dream of theirs to own or run a summer camp program.

Once I recovered from my surgery, I decided to go back to the workforce as an employee. I always got along with other people and treated people the way I wanted to be treated. But I found it hard to work for other companies because I felt it was a setback in my life to return to work after working for myself.

I became unhappy, and I witnessed the unfair treatment by employers toward their employees. There weren't enough team players within the company and many adults behaved worse than children in most cases. I was able to assess the type of upbringing some of these adults had by the way they interacted in the workforce.

No matter whom I worked for, I just did not feel a sense of belonging, and it wasn't because of the company. I just believed I was too intelligent to invest the time and labor to help make rich a company that was not my own. At the same time, I was truthful to myself, and I had to face my own reality, that without the courage of starting and operating my own business, without feeling a need to have partners, I will not be able to have my own business. I must go to work, and that is what I did. What I discovered about myself was I couldn't work long for any company. I did one to three years the most, but to spend half of my life working for someone else's company, I just couldn't see it happening for me.

After a year or two, I decided to do something with *Teens in Islam*. I learned a lot from our teenagers, their outlooks on life, and how they saw adults. With *Teens in Islam*, the purpose was to give these teens an outlet, but I realized the children of other religions could not participate in certain activities, and therefore, it was restricted to them. By doing this, I learned a lot about teens regardless of their beliefs; most teens find each other in school or in their own community.

Another thing I learned was parents of religion try to protect their children from the negative elements of society. Shaitan (Satan) always finds a way to get next to the weakest link in families, and in most cases, he targets the children. So *Teens in Islam* became a positive platform for teens. They even brought their friends to the program who weren't of the same faith but with whom they shared the same troubles and pressures.

Through this organization, we were able to publish articles written by teens pertaining to a variety of topics. We also enjoyed going on field trips, and it was the teenagers who brought about Teens of Georgia Temp Services because of their concerns, and the Muslim teens wanted to open it up to their non-Muslim friends. Each teen wanted to work; however, some teenagers were too young, and some teenagers were discouraged to work because employers had a lack of training dealing with teenagers.

In many of these cases, management already had a negative opinion of teens because of how the media views them. Teens don't share every problem or worry; each teen is unique in their own way. This particular project I had a great deal of interest in, and I took it to heart. Teens of Georgia became my non-profit organization because of my past experiences. I started Teens of Georgia without the help of anyone, and I did it at home. I realized for once in my life I wanted to do something on my own. That statement came from my dear mother, who always encouraged me to do things by myself. I did, but still after I got Teens of Georgia off the ground, I started bringing people in. It became a unique project, becoming the first temporary agency for teens. We offered more than job placement; we provided employment training as well as entrepreneur projects for teens who wanted to start their own business.

I enjoyed meeting with new companies that gave the teenagers a chance. They did not have to pay the company itself; the only thing I wanted them to do was to open the doors, giving the teenagers an opportunity to work for their company. Teens of Georgia helped build the teens' self-esteem, but one day my dreams were shattered.

I hired someone I knew who undermined me. I began to lose hope, and at some point, I stopped fighting. Regrets, yes! I regretted that I gave up. But I am grateful to Allah for opening my eyes. I always kept Allah out front. At the top of my letters was the heading "In the Name of Allah, The Most Merciful, The Mercy Giving." From day one, this was the way I started off when writing letters and proposals for years. I took the heading off because I got a complaint from within my organization—not from a parent, not from the companies who partnered with us, not from Kellogg Foundation, but from the person I hired who was my friend.

The day I unprotected the organization and myself, Shaitan (Satan) walked into Teens of Georgia.

I cried. I was angry and hurt, not only because of the person I allowed to come into my organization but also because I gave up on the children I took in for the summer. They weren't old enough to get a job but didn't want to be a part of the city summer programs. Since then, other non-profit organizations jumped on the bandwagon and that was good. We can never have enough programs to save our children from the ills of this society.

In September of 1999, a non-profit organization offered Teens of Georgia office space in return for placing their youth. At the same time, this organization was building a program similar to that of Teens of Georgia, which involved employment training and job placement. Teens of Georgia accepted the offer, and at the same time, I realized we would be helping another organization to build off Teens of Georgia's idea.

That's great! Once again, anything to save our youth. I may not gain financially, but I feel the blessing is far better than the money. For those people who want to go into a program that will benefit our youth, do research and see what you can offer and do differently. You will succeed; just don't give up or lose faith. Setbacks come with the business, and that's when you work even harder.

After fifteen years, I finally found my niche, and that is writing! My mother left me the greatest gift a mother can leave a child when they pass on, and that is words of encouragement along with beautiful memories. She would be proud to know I'm listening and living out her advice. With the help of Allah, I will succeed.

Please learn from my experiences, as well as the mistakes I made along the way. I have turned those oversights into positive influences. The best business experience is one that you learn yourself.

 **Yesterday you dared to struggle, but today you live to struggle . . . there is no experience in life without a struggle.**

If you have put your ideas together and you are ready to open up your halal business that is pleasing to Allah, let's get started.

# Chapter 2

## Let's Get Started

You must make a decision whether you're going to be a for-profit or non-profit business. There are three types of businesses: (1) proprietorship, (2) partnership, and (3) corporation.

**Proprietor**: a person having the exclusive title or legal right to something (an owner).

**Proprietorship**: the simplest and most basic type of business license where you are taxed as an individual. As a sole proprietor of your own operation, you reap the complete rewards of your efforts and your business.

**Partnership**: an association formed by contract between two or more competent persons to combine their money, capital, effects, labor and skill, or any or all of them, in lawful business or commerce and to share the profit and bear the loss in certain proportions. A partnership is a more complicated form of business than individual ownership. It does not matter how many people are partners with you (2–25), but there must be at least two.

A partnership begins with an agreement, which could be spoken or written as long as you and your partners have an understanding.

**Corporation**: an entity or artificial person created by law, consisting of one or more natural persons united in a body bearing a distinctive name. A corporation is endowed by law with the capacity of perpetual succession. That is, it remains the same though its members may die or change, and it is empowered to act as a unit or as a single individual.

The corporation is the third major form of business and by far the most important; most corporations are businesses operated for profit. There are also non-profit or non-stock corporations. Religions, charitable, and cooperative corporations are other types. With any business, you must find out what it will take to get your business started. In some cases, people will say they started their business with zero dollars, and in others, people have started with as little as a thousand dollars. We first must start from research, determining how much it will take to get started. Once you have done that, you can move on.

I used to think one can start their business with zero dollars, but the truth of the matter is, if you're going into business you will never start from zero; the only thing will cost you nothing is your idea. You will find out on that day you apply for licenses, you must pay for them, and when you incorporate your business, i.e., LLCs, you must pay to get a corporate certificate. The only thing will cost you zero dollars is the EIN, except when applying for a 501c3 tax exemption. Technically, you will never find a business starting with zero dollars if it's legal. I started my business off with zero dollars, I thought, and with a lot of support from friends who wanted me to succeed. It wasn't as easy as I had planned for it to be. I did research, and I asked myself, "What can I do that other businesses aren't doing?" This is where you must start.

The bottom line is, "What can you do better?" Nowadays, there are thousands of businesses out there that are of the same type. However, they have to do something different to bring customers in and keep customers coming to their business.

When I first started, I went sole proprietorship when I opened up the in-home day care. I started out with no *income* to operate this business. How was that possible? Because my home was already children-friendly, I had my own children, and they had toys, and I had food. I owned a typewriter and had paper, which allowed me to type up the rules and regulations. I ran an ad in the newspaper; during those days in the early '80s you paid for the ad later. Most importantly, when I first started off and I received my first payment in advance, it helped a lot. You will be surprised how much this will help you. You will be able to purchase some of the items or supplies you may need for your business. You can get families to donate safe toys or visit some of nurseries that will donate older toys that are still in good condition.

Even after you have discovered how much it will take to get started, take small steps and start working toward your business. Start buying supplies as you go along. Being in business by yourself means you are taking full responsibility for your actions, and you have no one to lay the blame on. Right now, it is easy to obtain a business license for some small businesses without too many restrictions, and you can purchase your business license and obtain your federal tax ID number. I would advise people who want to go into a business and have not yet purchased a building for this business, to at least secure the name, unless you're planning to have an at home-based businesses, since rules and regulations change all the time.

Like I said, it is easy to get a business license now, and there are not too many restrictions, but again this depends on the city and state in which you reside. Get your license as soon as possible and renew them yearly until you are able to get your business started. If you're opening a non-profit organization, work on getting your own 501-C3. This is a tax-exempt number for not-for-profit organizations. It is allowed in some states for another organization to carry your not-for-profit organization, if you don't have your 501c3 but are in operation. Today, many government-funded programs will not allow this action anymore if you're applying for your own funding.

They require that you have your own number. I found it to be helpful when I started with the summer camp. I went under the umbrella of another organization, they secured my funding, and they gave me the funding I needed. Although they were not the ones doing the program, they still had to account for the monies and report it to the IRS. So I advise people to get your own to keep unnecessary problems at a minimum, and in this case, you don't have to chase down others who receive the money for your organization. Lawyers usually charge $500 and up to complete your tax-exempt paperwork. If you are able to do it yourself, or get someone who is familiar to review it, you will save money. Your only out-of-pocket expense will be your filing fees. Once you are tax-exempt, you are eligible to apply for funding from federal and state grants that will fund your program.

Going into partnership? Condense it into writing. This will avoid a lot of confusion and anyone claiming to forget what one may have said verbally. Partnerships can work as long as you have a mutual agreement. I always tell people to find business partners who are of like nature.

In other words, don't go into business with a person whose interest is in lawn care when yours is in men's clothing. Find a partner who shares the same interests. It doesn't necessarily have to be a friend or relative; it can be someone you met at work who has similar business ideas as yours and shares the same values, morals, and principles. Keep the same rules with friends and family members when going into a partnership, and please make sure you share the same interests.

Establish a budget! A business that is starting out with zero dollars must record how much it will take to be operational.

This includes rent, utilities, paper, advertisement, and others. "I learned this would cost money. I may as well give up." Stop! *Where is your faith?* I'm a realist, and I know you can do it. Before I go on, let's remove some things from our vocabulary: *IF, BUT, I CAN'T*. These words can be negative.

Some of us are unable to get a loan because of our credit status. Some people's credit isn't bad; it's just too new, and there are creditors who are willing to give you a chance with a small loan. Once you secure your loan, remember to only spend on what you need. This is an opportunity to build your credit, and always put yourself in a position where you can pay it off before the interest kicks in. Remember never to get angry or give up if you are turned down. Today, creditors are giving secured credit cards that will help people who have bad, slow, or new credit opportunities to get established.

# Chapter 3

## Starting From Scratch

Starting from scratch is something we all must do. Some of us have money to get started, and some of us don't. This does not mean we can't start our business. What this does mean is that you must see what it will take to bring your idea into reality. Here are materials you will need to get started:

    a.  A sheet of paper
    b.  A pen/pencil

These items cost under $3 and can help you start from scratch if you don't own a computer. I realized not everyone owns a computer. Now I want you to write your ideas down on that sheet of paper. I'm here to tell you that working hard to develop your idea isn't easy, but don't be afraid to take a risk. Most successful businesses come from hard work and little income. You must make a decision whether or not you're ready to get started.

Most people today have access to a computer, enabling them to conduct their own research to see if their idea already exists. If you don't own a computer to access the Internet, go to a library and use their computers. You can even check out books that show ideas that have been patented. Once research reveals that your idea isn't or is on the market, don't stop, keep moving. I'm not telling you to quit your job, but *DO NOT* procrastinate! That is something we all are guilty of, one way or another. When you pause, the smartest person knows life still moves on while you are standing still.

When you finally decide to start moving with the clock again, someone has already moved forward with the same idea you visualized years ago. Let me share this short story with you. In the late '80s I had an idea about making this stroller for toddlers, I was so excited; I didn't have business people around me to say, "Get it patented, slow down, get a contract, have the right people work on it, secure it." Instead, I went to Atlanta Area Tech where I spoke with a professor about appointing a student to work on a prototype so I can get the stroller produced. I gave him my plans, and I never patented it, or sent a copy to myself; I didn't secure it at all. The professor told me to come back in two weeks and the students will have a prototype for me to review. I returned to the school, and he said the student left the school and never returned. There was nothing I could do about it. In the year 2000, I saw the stroller that I designed being pushed by a mother in a park. My advice to you: never give up on your ideas. If you don't have the money to develop it, secure it at least!

What I want you to do is spend one hour per day working on your project. Make this your relaxation period. Do you know what I mean? This is like the TV "hour" where people spend three hours in front of the tube relaxing, watching their favorite TV show.

If you can't turn off that television during the time that you need to work on your project, then get on your computer while your program is on and start working and/or write information down on paper. Eventually, you will discover you can hear your program. It's like music; in many cases, you listen to the radio, but you don't see the singer. This message is for serious people only!

Now we are going to take one of those hours for developing those ideas. On the same sheet of paper, I want you to answer the following questions:

1.  Is this a home-based business?
2.  Have you picked out a name?     ·
3.  What type of business, i.e., corporation, LLC, company, self-employed?
4.  Have you done a cost analysis?
5.  Do you have a budget?
6.  Have you done the research on your project?
7.  Is this for profit or non-profit?
8.  Will your idea benefit others?
9.  Does it need to be manufactured?
10. Is it marketable? (What I mean by "marketable" is, is this something that you will go out of your way to purchase?)
11. Is it worth the time, effort, and energy to have it patented?
12. How much time are you willing to spend on this product a day?

There are many non-profit organizations out there that will help you make the right decisions or guide you when starting up a business. Please check out your local Small Business Association (SBA).

In many cases, people do not have the start-up money. I found myself with excellent ideas; I didn't have the funds to get the business off the ground. Most times, people would share their ideas with a person who has the money, but he or she is not willing to invest in the idea or become a partner to get that idea off the ground. For me, I have mentioned my ideas to others who had the money to invest but didn't, and what they did do? They took my idea and put it into action. The issue that they faced was they didn't have the formula to that idea—I did, guess what? It wasn't for sale.

This is when you must trust people who are willing to invest or loan or are willing to go into business with you. If not, you must depend on yourself.

This brings me to raising funds to get your business off the ground.

If you have a name for your business and your product, then secure the name. There are many ways you can secure the name for your business, but you must research to make sure no one else has the same name.

You must decide on what type of business you are going to operate using the information given to you above. Once you've decided whether you're going to be a for-profit or nonprofit, LLC, C-corporation, or D-corporation, then you can obtain your business license as well as your EIN (employment identification number).

## Raising Funds to Start Your Business

If you need funds to start a business, there are several ways to do this without fundraising. You can take a part-time job or you can look for investors or find an interest-free loan. Once you reach this decision, it's best to know what you must do to raise the funds. Some organizations offer block grants or minority loans.

## What To Expect?

As with any business, everyone expects to succeed. Think about your long-term goals and short-term goals. Don't rush into anything; you will learn that with any business you will have slow periods and fast periods.

Let's talk about sales. During a certain time of year, there are products that will sell extremely well. For example, T-shirts. You will find that T-shirts sell better during the summer months, and there are some products that sell all year round, such as household products, i.e., cleaning powder.

My best advice to you is when you have a product that is moving at a fast pace, always keep enough money set aside to cover your expenses. This includes salaries you must pay out during your slow production period. When your business can take care of its own during your slow months, you have nothing to worry about. Remember, don't expect something for nothing. As the old saying goes, "nothing in life is free."

Not everyone is going to be for your business or about your business. Don't expect people you have known your entire life to support you. This does not mean these individuals don't care about you or don't want to see you prosper. It's just a part of life; not everyone shares the same sentiments. What I do know is if you depend on these individuals to support you and your endeavor, you will likely be disappointed. Tell them about your business; let them decide to support you without you begging for it. As with anything, you will learn whom you can and cannot count on for support.

Everyone I know, including my family and friends, always tell me I come up with excellent ideas, and one day I would be rich. I even have some friends who stand by my side no matter what type of idea I come up with as long as it's lawful. I knew the ones who were there for me and the ones who weren't. All this was made clear, and it was left up to me to decide which of these individuals I can call on for support.

I found myself, as I stated earlier, including everyone in my dreams. It wasn't that I didn't believe in myself; I just wanted the best for everyone. I wanted people I cared about to be on the bandwagon in the beginning just in case I hit it big. I love my family and friends, and this is my way of showing them that. Until one day, my mother said,

"Baby, stop giving everything away. There is a reason that you're not a millionaire." I heard her, but I felt she really didn't understand. Now I realize I was the one who didn't understand.

It took my mother's passing for me to see and appreciate exactly what she was saying to me. Truly, in business we all want to succeed, and I am here to tell you success starts from within and you must want it. Just because you are a part of your family's and friends' lives doesn't mean you are a part of theirs.

Move forward, this is your idea, and remember, this is the vision Allah has given to you, and He gives to whomever He pleases. Your foresight is not everyone else's vision.

## A Need?

This is a question asked by most people. "Is there a need for this type of business?" When you come up with an idea, ask yourself whether you would buy or support this type of business. Most likely your answer will be yes because this is your idea. I don't care if there are one hundred day care centers out there; there is always room for more. It is not so much a need as it is a want. It has to do with what you can offer your clients, contrary to what the other day care centers can't.

Use your own judgment about a need. Not only can you do it, you can also do it even better. This is the affirmation you must tell yourself! You are your own unique person, and only you can implement your idea. When I started the teen programs, I knew there was a need. When I came up with Teens of Georgia, I researched newspapers on a daily, weekly, and monthly basis. Crimes committed by teenagers were on the rise, and it was clear that there was a need for more teenager programs.

This applies to children as well. There will always be a need for improvement in any business. Other companies come about because they see a need for improvement.

## Family

Your family can be either your worst clients or your best supporters. You must first realize this is your family. Shaitan's entire mission is to divide the family, and I know you've heard it over and over: "Don't do business with family. Don't hire family members." It's just like hearing, "Don't do business with Black people or don't trust White people." Then the worst is when you hear, "Don't do business with people that you worship with or those you attend religious service with." These are the "whisperers"; each family member is unique and is not necessarily a bad person to do business with or to even have work for you, and not every White or Black person or person you attend worship with is bad. Stop letting Shaitan divide you. Know that if you are a human being, you will deal with trial and error, and in some cases, you may fall in the same boat where people just might say, "Don't do business with him or her." We all have a little voice in us that makes us think twice or think wrong. We must stop letting the whispers divide us from family, people, and community when doing business. Stop getting upset when your family doesn't support you or agree with you. You offer something, and these things are not free, be they products or services. When your family comes to you for handouts, you must separate the two, i.e., business and family. Don't give anything you can't afford to let go of. Only people who care about you and your business will understand when you say, "I'm not in a position to give anything away. However, when I'm able to do so, I will let you know."

Families are life friends. They're either going to be supportive or not. This doesn't mean you don't have a good business; it just means you have learned to separate the two for the sake of family and friendship.

Get your family involved by asking for their ideas. Ask them to help push your business even if it's just by giving out business cards. In some cases, you can give your family members discounts for assisting you. Sometimes, it's easy for family members to understand your business when you share the ins and outs of the day-to-day activities (costs, profits, and losses). Most times, family and friends think your business is very successful when you get a new car or house. But what they do not see is the behind the scenes, the debt that goes with getting the new house or new car, and frankly you do not have to share this information with your family. Just be careful of those family members who are not supportive at all; their actions show. Therefore, don't try to get them to see what they don't want to see or understand what they don't want to understand. Just continue being nice and kind at a distance especially when Allah has revealed how they truly feel about you and your business. Family members can be supportive even if it's just by giving words of encouragement. Just remember, your family is people too!

## Salat (Prayer)

Allah is Most Merciful. Behind all success is the Will of Allah. Your business can go a long way with faith and trust in Allah. Keep the faith and keep praying. You will learn through trial and error, still Allah will not let you down. Keep going and believe in Him. When you find yourself in a bind due to a mistake on your part or even a faulty decision by others, keep in mind that Allah is still there.

Continue to pray for success. Come to success, come to success, come to prayer. I say this a lot because I know it can be very challenging to be consistent in offering your prayers. With that in mind, it's equally as hard to be unfailing in your business endeavors. Nevertheless, when you put Allah first in your life and are persistent in prayer, you will strive just as hard for your business.

Do you ask Allah for things that you don't believe in? Do you ask Allah for something you don't work toward yourself? These questions are important; first, you will not ask Allah for something that you yourself do not believe in. How can you ask Allah to bless you with a good idea, then when He does, you doubt that idea and/or you don't believe that it's Allah answering your prayers. And if you do believe that Allah answered your prayers, then why aren't you working on that idea yourself? We must learn to trust in Allah and in ourselves; good comes from Allah and wrong comes from within.

**Brainstorm**

I've been brainstorming for a long time trying to decide how I want to sell this book. With anything you must brainstorm, but don't get caught up brainstorming too much. You will get burnt out. However, brainstorming helps when you find yourself in financial trouble. Making the right decision about your business is important. You must realize this is your business. Put all your thoughts on paper, look your thoughts over, and see what is best for your business.

Imagine writing information on many types of pads and trying to decide which direction to go. Well, that's me. I have written down idea after idea, brainstorming how and when I will put my next project into effect. Well, guess what? You are reading it. This is my project to write and make it effective for people who want to move forward in their lives and to make a difference not just in their lives but in others' lives as well.

Interesting facts: The only thing that will keep you alive is Allah, because He is the giver of life and death! So don't get angry at my opinions and my own storylines and facts from the government census. The truth is, to make this world a better place we must take back our world from the evil within it, by saying *NO* to what Allah has asked us to stay away from, for it will harm our souls.

"Save yourselves and your family from the Hellfire." [insert source] What is the Hellfire? The disbelievers will soon discover what all the Prophets (peace be upon them all) were talking about, from Prophet Abraham to Prophet Muhammad (peace be upon them).

And for those men and women who believe that Muslims are the worst people, follow the money trail and see who truly are the worst of people and why. And if you find some Muslims such as the people who are going against Allah's Laws like those of other faiths, then you know they too are disbelievers.

What is crazy is that I have to apologize to White and Black Americans for Muslim behavior when all races commit hideous crimes against people.

Why do some Americans want to destroy the image of true righteous Muslims? That's the question. And why do some Americans want to destroy the image of their own people? Ask that question. It's the fight between evil and good, is it? Or is it about *GREED*?

This book is only to assist us in focusing on saving our world, starting right here on the land in which my mother gave birth to me and raised me—America!

Feel free to write me at P.O. Box 312264 Atlanta, GA 31131.

Do right by Allah; don't let your own evil desires destroy your relationship with Allah!

I am striving to get into *PARADISE* and it's not here on *EARTH*! I do believe this. I am striving to get the good of this life and I pray it will benefit me in the next!